Esm
glim

Mitch stared at the drop. It was right...*there*. He could just lick it off. It would be a favor....

As he silently debated precisely how she would taste, her gaze suddenly jerked upward.

"Oh! Look! There!" She pointed and he managed to catch the fading wisp of a falling star.

The sight of her lips parted with excitement did something to him. Made his heart pound and his blood take a fast trip south. He felt full of wild urges he had to act on or he'd explode.

He had to kiss her.

He leaned over the table, his chair creaking under the strain, cupped the back of her head and pressed his lips to hers.

Like a match rasping across a phosphorus strip, he felt an explosive heat, sharp, bright and hot. Hell, he felt like a star shooting across the sky above them.

All he wanted was more.

Blaze™

Dear Reader,

I'm sorry to say goodbye to the DOING IT...BETTER! miniseries. But since Esmeralda predicted happily-ever-afters for her friends, I was delighted to finally give Esmeralda hers.

I spent most of my life avoiding all psychics. Why? Fear that they might reveal to me a terrible fate that would negatively affect my life. Yet psychic characters popped up regularly in my stories. Eventually, I overcame my reluctance and visited three recommended psychics. The experiences were remarkable—like purposeful therapy. Guess what I learned. My fate is in my hands. Surprised?

I must thank two online communities—Psychic Living and Palmistry Primal Focus—for countless insights and guidance. My gratitude is boundless to Australian palmist Susanne Macrae for her dead-on feedback and advice on what my characters' palms might reveal.

As Mitch and Esmeralda faced the issues of fate versus free will and trusting your own instincts, I learned valuable lessons myself. I hope you do, too. I'd love to hear from you! Write me at dawn@dawnatkins.com.

Happy reading,
Dawn Atkins

AT HIS FINGERTIPS
Dawn Atkins

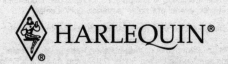

HARLEQUIN®

TORONTO • NEW YORK • LONDON
AMSTERDAM • PARIS • SYDNEY • HAMBURG
STOCKHOLM • ATHENS • TOKYO • MILAN • MADRID
PRAGUE • WARSAW • BUDAPEST • AUCKLAND

ISBN-13: 978-0-373-79322-8
ISBN-10:   0-373-79322-7

AT HIS FINGERTIPS

ABOUT THE AUTHOR

Dawn Atkins started her writing career in the second grade crafting stories that included every single spelling word her teacher gave her. Since then, she's expanded her vocabulary and her publishing credits. This book is her eighteenth published book. She won the 2005 Golden Quill for Best Sexy Romance and has been a *Romantic Times BOOKreviews* Reviewers' Choice Award finalist for Best Flipside (2005) and Best Blaze (2006). She lives in Arizona with her husband, teenage son and a butterscotch-and-white cat. She knows just enough about palm reading to be dangerous and she's not exactly psychic, but she's been told she has a wildly sunny aura.

Books by Dawn Atkins

HARLEQUIN BLAZE
93—FRIENDLY PERSUASION
155—VERY TRULY SEXY
176—GOING TO EXTREMES
205—SIMPLY SEX
214—TEASE ME
253—DON'T TEMPT ME...*
294—WITH HIS TOUCH†
306—AT HER BECK AND CALL†

HARLEQUIN TEMPTATION
871—THE COWBOY FLING
895—LIPSTICK ON HIS COLLAR
945—ROOM...BUT NOT BORED!
990—WILDE FOR YOU

HARLEQUIN FLIPSIDE
11—A PERFECT LIFE?

HARLEQUIN DUETS
77—ANCHOR THAT MAN!
91—WEDDING FOR ONE
    TATTOO FOR TWO

*Forbidden Fantasies
†Doing It...Better!

To my friend Suzan,
for opening her heart and my eyes

1

"So if I want this grant, I should let you read my palm?" The young woman bumped the table with a knee, sloshing the gingko-chamomile tea Esmeralda McElroy had brewed to enhance alertness and calm for her and her clients.

"It's not a requirement, hon. Consider it a bonus gift." Esmeralda zeroed in on Cindy's face. Something was wrong with Cindy's grant application and Esmeralda had to figure out what. Esmeralda's psychic skills weren't a formal part of her job as director of the Dream A Little Dream Foundation, but they were the reason she'd been hired after the first director left. Olivia, the founder, had been a palm client and trusted Esmeralda implicitly.

The proposal for an exercise playland for toddlers was solid, but as Cindy explained the benefits of large-muscle development and parent-child bonding, her eyes were empty, her aura gray with gloom. Cindy had a dream, but it wasn't this one.

"A gift? And this will help?" Cindy bit her lip.

"I could read tea leaves if you prefer." Esmie had recently ordered some silver-needle tea that produced dramatic configurations. "Your aura is as gray as a rain cloud."

"My aura is…gray?" Cindy blinked at her.

"Let's stick with your palm, huh?" Esmeralda smiled kindly.

Cindy extended a hesitant hand and when Esmeralda cupped it, she felt a rough spot on Cindy's left thumb. "Cuticles need a trim." She paused, then spoke in the somber voice of a TV fortune-teller. "Through my crystal ball…I see in your future…a healing manicure." She grinned. "I do nails, too."

"Really?" Cindy laughed, relaxing as Esmie had hoped. It was no accident that her own aura was wild with light-hearted yellow.

"I love this." Cindy touched Esmie's index fingernail, which held the stenciled star with a rhinestone fleck she'd created for the thirty-fifth birthdays of her and her friends.

"Thanks. So…let's see what's going on with you, hmm?" She took Cindy's hand again, closed her eyes, silently prayed for clarity and wisdom, then looked down at Cindy's earth hand with its square palm and short, evenly spaced fingers.

The girl's heart line held passion, but the angle of her thumb showed she was not ambitious…hmm.

Cindy's story came together in Esmie's head, clicking into place like puzzle pieces. "Ah… I get it."

"You do?" Cindy said. "You get it?"

"You want to work with kids, Cindy, but not in a business, as a teacher. Here is your passion…" She pointed to the line. "This shows how you lead by example. This shows your need to interact with people. You're a natural teacher."

Cindy gave a sad smile. "But I only have one semester at Phoenix College."

"That's easy to fix. Request a scholarship from us." Esmeralda tapped the grant application. "Whose dream is this?"

The girl flushed. "My dad's. He read about childhood obesity and how yuppie parents hover over their kids, so he thought this would be a moneymaker."

"He's right, I'm sure, but you need to overcome your tendency to please others, sometimes to your own detriment. Use the courage that's here." She touched the large, curved upper Mars mount.

"That's my courage?" She looked so hopeful.

"Absolutely. Tomorrow night I'm holding a Wish Upon A Star workshop. We help people pin down dreams and make them real. I think you and your dad should come."

"My dad?"

"Sure. So he can own this dream—" she patted the application "—and understand yours."

"Okay. We'll come. Thanks." Cindy beamed, then looked down at her hand. "You see anything else I should know?"

Before Esmeralda finished, Cindy had a plan to declare her independence from her father, an appointment for a full reading—and a manicure—and tears in her eyes.

Esmeralda accepted Cindy's hug and said goodbye, pleased, but drained. Back-to-back appointments, someone's dreams on the line every hour, was exhausting. But this was only week four. Surely she'd build stamina.

She had to make time to read through the grant applications on her desk—two daunting towers of spiral binders, portfolios and folders. She should work weekends, too, except her palm and nail clients needed her.

This week she had to hire a consultant to make sense of the jumbled business plan she'd inherited. Lack of business expertise was her Achilles heel, but she wouldn't let that stop her. Phoenix was a mecca for entrepreneurs and people starting over. She should have no trouble finding a consultant.

Thinking of all she faced made the knot in her chest tighten and her stomach churn, but she would make this work. The Dream A Little Dream Foundation was a once-in-a-lifetime chance to make a difference in lots of lives. She loved reading palms, of course, but sometimes it seemed like such an insubstantial thing. The foundation was big and tangible and important.

It would make her mother proud, too. As a dedicated social worker and counselor, her mother had always given so much to her own clients. She was Esmie's hero. This job was a way to follow in her mother's footsteps, to honor her memory.

Needing energy, Esmie bent into a fan pose, legs apart, elbows to the floor, and eased into a refreshing stretch.

"So, it went well?" The voice of her assistant, Belinda Warwick, made Esmeralda jump up so fast she had to grab her desk for balance.

"It did. Yes. Once I read her palm and saw what she needed." That success reassured Esmie that she belonged here. A person without her skills might have funded the well-crafted proposal without noticing the disconnect between the dreamer and the dream. The purpose of the foundation was not just to give out money, it was to fulfill dreams.

"I wish I had a thimble-full of your talent," Belinda said. "I study, but it doesn't get through." She tapped her temple with the nail on which she'd had Esmeralda stencil the star design, making her many bracelets rattle. She'd asked where Esmeralda bought hers and doubled the number she wore.

"It takes time, Belinda. Hundreds of readings, hours of study. You can't rush it."

Esmeralda had inherited Belinda, Olivia's niece, who aspired to be a palm reader. She saw herself as Esmeralda's protégée and took notes on everything Esmie did, practically giving an "I'm not worthy" bow when she left the room. Esmeralda feared Belinda's hero worship kept her from picking up her own inner voice, which was crucial for success.

"Your four o'clock had to reschedule," Belinda said. "I wasn't able to get a fill-in."

"That's fine. Gives me time to catch up." She nodded at the towers of proposals.

"We're still getting calls from the newspaper article."

"That's good." A feature in the *Arizona Republic* about the foundation had tripled the calls and applications. The story had even been picked up by papers outside Phoenix.

"I'd be happy to go through these," Belinda said, looking through the top few.

"Let's see how it goes." Belinda knew even less than she did about grants and business. Esmeralda had to blaze a trail first.

"I'd love to help…really." Her voice faded as she flipped through the stack. "Tomorrow, your nine o'clock is a man you know…."

"Really?" Esmeralda's heart jumped. Could it be Jonathan at last? Was her ex-husband finally showing up as predicted? *You must begin anew with a man from your past* were the exact words from three separate readings. Their marriage had ended abruptly and she blamed herself, so a second chance was perfect.

Belinda's gaze shot to her. "Oh, wait. I'm sorry. It's not the man from your past. At first, when he said he knew you, my heart flipped, too, but he's a bartender from Moons. Jasper?"

"Oh, sure." Esmeralda knew him through a hairdresser at her shop who also waitressed at the strip club. Before Jasper could start the stock group he wanted a grant for, he had to control the gambling impulse she'd read in his hand.

"I'm so sorry it wasn't him." Belinda had done one of the readings that picked up *the man from her past* message and seemed to feel responsible for his arrival. Esmeralda hadn't mentioned Jonathan to Belinda—she was embarrassed enough about how eagerly she kept an eye out for the familiar dimples, the blond thatch and the big smile of her ex-husband. She really missed him. And she was dying to see him.

"He'll get here when the time is right," she said, showing a patience she didn't feel.

"Shall I smudge your office?" Belinda asked. "Make some tea? Light your incense?"

"I'm fine, Belinda. Truly." Belinda behaved as though *assistant* was code for *slave*. Absolutely not Esmeralda's way. "Don't you have a reading in a bit?" Belinda used Esmie's salon station to see a few clients. "Why don't you take off early?"

"Are you sure? I really want to help in any way I can."

"You are helping. You've got the appointment calendar just right. The grant evaluation rubric and spread-sheet look great. The Web site's coming along. The biggest thing is getting the books straight."

Belinda cringed, ducking her head. "That. Right. I got some help from a friend of mine? Rico? If that's okay? He did the books for Uncle Louis, so he's showing me the basics."

"Sounds like a plan." She'd never met him, but if Rico worked for Olivia's brother, he'd be trustworthy. She had some vague recollection that Rico and Belinda had dated, too. "So go. Leave early. Study the palms I gave you." She'd given her several photos with interpretation for training purposes.

"If you're sure?" When Esmie nodded, Belinda bounded away, her bracelets jingling, blond curls bouncing. She'd bleached and curled her hair to match Esmeralda's. Wore similar clothes, too. Esmeralda found it embarrassing—and potentially disturbing—but she knew from Belinda's palm that she needed a role model to develop security. Esmeralda would do her best to be that person.

She headed into her office for a head-clearing meditation.

Her cell stopped her. It was Annika, her temporary roommate, with an update. One of Esmie's foster dogs had bitten a hole in the sofa she was holding for a friend; Esmie's neighbor wanted to borrow her car; two friends needed advice; three people wanted palm appointments.

Sometimes Esmeralda's life felt so full it seemed ready to pop, but giving felt too good to have regrets. The universe never gave you more than you could handle.

To clear her head for reviewing grants, she warmed her strawberry-scented shoulder bag in the microwave, lit strawberry incense, put *Yoga Chill* on her CD player, and hefted herself into a legs-up-the-wall pose.

She laid the steamy, sweet-smelling bag across her face so it rested on either side of her head, blocking all but a whisper of music. Air brushed her bare legs, since her skirt had fallen to her lap.

She breathed in slowly through her nose, out through her mouth, letting her thoughts gather one by one.

They were mostly worries. Could she nail the business aspects of the work? Would she make good grant choices? Would she impress the board at the first meeting? Olivia had hinted some board members were skeptical about Esmeralda's skills. Would she even be ready in a month?

As each worry arose, she pictured a fat, fluffy cloud lifting it away across the blue sky of her mind. What about Jonathan? That was a hope, not a worry, at least.

She'd almost called him in San Diego, the last address she had. But she knew she should let the universe churn, not try to wrestle the prediction into what she wanted—her tendency. As with many psychics, readings on herself or those she loved were rarely accurate, consisting of wishful thinking and selective omissions. *He'll appear when he's supposed to,* she told herself and let a gold-tinted cloud float Jonathan away.

IT WAS NEARLY FIVE when Mitch Margolin stepped into the Dream A Little Dream Foundation office. The walls were purple with gold trim and covered with posters with woo-woo slogans. There were crystals on a table and stars everywhere—star mobiles, star paintings, star paperweights, even stars in a small water fountain. Full on fairy dust.

And it sank his hope like a stone.

Damn. He wanted a solid opportunity for his brother, not mystical nonsense. He'd even called his buddy Craig with the Attorney General's office to see if there was anything suspicious about the foundation, which sounded too good to be true.

For now, Mitch was here to learn what he could. If the place was for real, it would be good to be an early applicant. Besides, Dale might lose interest any minute. His brother was a bass player who contented himself with what he made playing gigs, teaching lessons or doing studio work. The fact he'd actually expressed interest in a day job made Mitch jump on it.

The empty desk and dark computer monitor told him the receptionist had gone for the day. Not long ago, though, judging by the smell of blown-out candles. A different, fruit-scented smoke came from deeper in the office. Incense?

He followed the smell down a short hall to a closed door. The nameplate said the office belonged to Esmeralda McElroy, Executive Director. He heard Eastern music—a sitar, cymbals and high-pitched singing—coming from inside.

Bookshelves beside the door held a peculiar mix of titles: *Tarot and You, What Color is Your Parachute? Small Business Basics, Palmistry for Beginners.* Business and New Age. More BS alarms went off in his attorney brain. Maybe he'd spent too much time around Craig, who had lots of con artist war stories—Phoenix was a hotbed for scammers—or maybe he'd seen enough rip-offs in his day.

Still, Mitch wanted this for his brother so badly he could taste it. It was Mitch's fault, after all, that Dale's life had never taken off, that, at thirty, the man lived like a teenager.

He tapped at the door. No answer. The music must be too loud, so he turned the knob and stepped inside.

He took in the busy room, painted in the same purple and gold as the reception area. Colorful artwork filled the walls, and the furniture was red and puffy and included a couple of star-covered beanbags. Above the spindly teak desk, he spotted something amiss—a pair of female legs sticking up, soles pointed at the ceiling.

O-o-o-oka-a-a-a-y.

She was doing some funky exercise—tai chi, yoga, whatever. He stepped close enough to speak to her, absently noting the stars on her toenails.

Her legs were shapely and tan and her colorful skirt had pooled at her hips, barely, uh, covering…uh. Mitch got an involuntary charge. He jerked his gaze where it belonged—to her face, which was covered by a bag.

He cleared his throat. "Excuse me?"

The woman startled, shoved the bag off her face and smiled at him from the floor, not the least embarrassed about her legs sticking up like that. "Hello there."

"Sorry to catch you…indisposed." He cleared his throat.

With a graceful move, she pushed away from the wall and down to a sit, legs crossed beneath her. "May I help you?"

"I hope so—" Whoa. Seeing her right side up, he was

startled to realize that he knew her. It was those eyes—an electric blue-green that almost hurt to look at.

They'd met years ago at a summer fair where his band had played. He'd been just out of college. She'd just graduated from high school and was learning to read palms. He'd let her read his—a play to get those fingers on him, her sweet breath close, her hot eyes right there. She'd studied his hand as if it was a secret map to all the world's riches.

Now she held out her hand so he could help her up. Her grip was firm and warm, and she sprang to her feet like a gymnast.

"You're Lady E," he said softly, still feeling the electricity of that brief contact.

Her exotic eyes went wide, her brow creased and both thin straps of her slippery top slid down her arms.

"You knew me then?" She hadn't recognized him, but that was no surprise. He'd long ago ditched the bleached-blond ponytail, goatee and thin 'stash. He shaved, kept his brown hair short and wore glasses.

"Wait… May I?" She reached for his wire frames and he let her tug them from his face. "Oh. Wow. You're Doctor X!"

From Xtent of the Crime, his band. So ridiculous, but at the time he'd been deadly serious and preposterously ambitious.

"I recognize your eyes," she said.

He had dime-a-dozen brown eyes, he knew, but he smiled all the same. "I'm Mitch Margolin." He took back his glasses, needing the barrier.

"Esmeralda McElroy," she said faintly, still staring.

"I can't believe you're here. After seventeen years... almost to the day."

"You remember the *day?*" It had been a great night and all, with a meteor shower, and making out had been hot, but still...

"That's because...well, another reason. Never mind." Pain crossed her face, but she forced a smile. "The point is, you're back in my life now."

"Back in your life?" Her words made him uneasy.

"You've changed," she said. "You look so different."

"And you look the same." She'd grown into her face, but her features were still fresh and young and sweet. Her puffy lips were parted softly. Her hair was still long, wavy and blond, tousled in that fresh-from-sex way he'd liked. A crystal on a thin cord rested easily in the hollow at the base of her throat and her collarbone looked so delicate it would snap in a hug. She took a shaky breath and those damnable straps shivered against her upper arms.

Her scent filled his head. Fresh, with a tart sweetness—like flowers and strawberries and oranges, like falling face first into a fruit and flower stand.

As she stared at him, he had the same eerie feeling he'd had that night—that she could see straight into him.

Had to be those eyes.

Or maybe he was caught up in leftover romantic impulses from his silent crush on Julie, his associate.

"Let's sit down and catch up." Esmeralda led him to an overstuffed couch, jingling as she padded, barefoot, across the room. The sound came from bracelets on both wrists and beads around her ankles. Still the same flower child, evidently.

The sofa was so soft he'd need a boost to climb out.

Esmeralda sat close, one leg caught under her, and her neckline drooped.

He averted his gaze, which snagged on her toes, but that seemed just as intimate. Hell, he didn't know where to look.

"So, how did you find me?" she asked eagerly, leaning forward, making those straps shiver against her skin.

"Find you?" Like he'd hunted her down? "I wasn't looking. I mean, it was the newspaper story. My brother read it. He has this idea for a grant, see, and—"

"Oh. The article." She seemed disappointed. "Oh, well. It got you here. The universe has its own sweet plan."

What the hell was she talking about? "Anyway, my brother Dale is a musician, and—"

"I remember. He was in your band. Extent of something…"

"Xtent of the Crime, yeah."

"Where are you playing now?"

"We broke up years ago. Just a few days after that night, actually. But Dale still plays and—"

"But you had that record deal. And I remember I saw in your palm that you would succeed."

Didn't she know how stupid that sounded?

"The L.A. thing didn't work out." They'd been scouted for a music video and three-album deal in L.A. In his gut, he'd known it was too easy, but when Lady E had read his palm—really, his wild hope—he'd been convinced to go for it. He'd been arrogant and ambitious, like every other twentysomething with a band.

She'd meant no harm. He'd been young, hooked by her sureness, the fire in her eyes, and ignored what his head told him.

"That's a shame. You were so good."

He'd played one of his songs for her, he remembered, and she'd stared, those eyes going from his face to his fingers and back, enthralled. What an ego boost.

"I grew up." And thank God for that. His first job out of law school had allowed him to bail his parents out of the dot-com crash, where they'd lost most of their investments.

"What do you do now?" Esmeralda asked.

"I'm an attorney. I practice business law. I'm a sole proprietor with an associate. I mostly work with startups."

"That's a long way from music. But there was lots of space between your heart and head lines, which means a strong commitment to fairness. And your lines were deep, I think, which means you're practical and grounded, like an attorney needs to be. But your head line had a creativity curve and I don't remember a split fate line. May I…?" She reached for his hand. "I have a great memory for palms."

Jesus. Palm reading had been fun at eighteen, but she was, what, thirty-five now? To his thirty-nine. "You're still into that…psychic stuff?"

"Of course." She blinked at him. "I was just learning when we met. I made some mistakes." Pain crossed her face again. "Maybe I was wrong when I read yours." She leaned forward for his hand again.

He withdrew it. "No big deal," he said, not wanting to laugh at her. "I didn't take it seriously."

"I do," she said. "I take it very seriously. It's my life's work."

"You're kidding." The words were out before he could figure out something more diplomatic. "I mean, you've got Executive Director by your name. You don't get a job like that reading crystal balls." He smiled, hoping to hell he was right. Think of the harm she could do to any poor schmuck who took her guesses at face value.

She'd been earnest when they'd met. Wide-eyed and full of hope. He'd been that way, too, really. Didn't miss it one bit. Hated that sense of expectation, that vulnerability and the crash that followed. Better to nail down what you wanted, set reasonable goals, then work to get them.

"The woman who started the foundation is one of my palmistry clients, and she asked me to apply for the job after the first director left."

"Really? Because you read her palms?"

"Really," she said, sounding insulted.

He had to smooth it. "But you had to have relevant experience." God, he hoped so, or his brother's grant was gone in a wisp of fruit-scented smoke.

"I have the credentials that matter to her."

"You mean a strong intuition, an understanding of human psychology, right? Personnel directors are like that." Was she a complete nut case? Or was it the founder who was crazy?

"It might interest you to know that there are scientific studies on palmar dermatoglyphics that have appeared in prominent professional journals." Her voice had an angry edge. "They have verified the link between hand markings and behavior. I can give you Web links or printouts if you—"

"I'm sorry. I got us off on the wrong foot. I came here to find out about a grant for my brother. I don't mean to offend you." Pissing off the CEO would not score a grant.

She sighed. "You're just not what I expected." She caught herself, covered her mouth. "I mean, remembered. But here you are. And on our anniversary. So that's that. We go from here."

"Where are we going?" He felt as though he'd fallen down some *Alice in Wonderland* rabbit hole.

"Don't you think it's curious that we're meeting again on exactly this day?" Maybe it wasn't incense he smelled. Maybe she'd been smoking some fruit-flavored hallucinogen.

"Small world, I guess." He moved his shoulders uneasily.

Her eyes found his with their strange piercing power, so he looked down, but there were her sloppy straps and her nipples.

Ouch.

"That was a magical night. Remember the meteor shower?"

"Sure. I guess."

"And the fruit we ate? Strawberries and raspberries and, my favorite, star fruit."

"It tasted like pears?" That was how she'd tasted. Like pears and something sweet that was all her. Her lips had been soft and strong, and he'd been so hot for her he thought he would explode—

"So, Mitch…?" She touched his hand.

Electricity zoomed through him. Seventeen years had gone by, but the chemistry between them had not changed one bit. *Screw the grant, screw her craziness,* he thought, blood pounding through him. He wanted this woman. Right here, right now.

2

"WHY DON'T YOU TELL ME about your brother's idea?"
Esmeralda managed to ask, trying not to sound stunned.
How could she help it, though? Doctor X had returned
seventeen years later, almost to the day of when they'd
met. The minute she recognized him, heat and light had
poured through her from the soles of her feet to every
last follicle on her scalp.

Mitch seemed stunned, too. By her touch or something in her gaze. Maybe some latent psychic impulse?
She could only hope.

There was attraction, of course. It shivered in the air
between them, like heat from an oven on broil, and
made her forget his insulting hints that she was in over
her head with the foundation.

Could he be the one? He was from the past, all right,
and they had unfinished business. He hadn't called her
when he'd returned from L.A. as he'd promised. But
then her life had changed so terribly the next day that a
hot musician from a star-mad night had faded to nothing
in her mind.

"His idea…?" Mitch seemed to struggle to clear his
head. "For the grant, right. It's, uh, a high school program to get low-income kids instruments and lessons.

He'll use musicians he knows to donate time and get a break on instruments…."

He kept explaining, while Esmeralda pondered possibilities. But he wasn't even Doctor X anymore. He was Mitch Margolin, attorney-at-law, and he'd sneered at her gift. When she'd asked to see his palm, he'd practically hidden it behind his back. He thought she was a crackpot.

How could he be the one? Her body seemed intrigued, that was certain. If she were fur-bearing, she'd be fluffed out like a puff ball, prickling with awareness.

That long ago night, her attraction had been so hot and bright it had almost hurt. Of course, she'd been a virgin and he was older *and* a musician *and* devastatingly hot. How could she not be smitten?

He was still exceptionally attractive, though his jaw seemed firmer, the planes of his face more chiseled. The eyes behind the fashionable glasses had gone from a soft brown to hard, dark marbles with pinpoints of white judgment in the center.

The ponytail that had made him seem laid back had been replaced by a crisp business cut, and his hair was a muted brown. His smile was still sexy, but it didn't seem to come so easily any more. Where he'd been wiry, he was now muscular and he smelled of a pricey cologne instead of sandalwood, clean sweat and fresh grass. The effect was serious, commanding, driven.

She felt funny sitting near him. Nervous, scared and, well…

Hot. She shifted against the ache between her legs, the rolling heat, the helpless urge to touch him, to be touched by him.

This was not how she expected to feel when the man

from her past appeared. Jonathan had made her feel relaxed and content. They'd been friends as well as lovers. With Mitch she felt jumpy, unsettled, irritable. And she ached all over.

"Esmeralda?"

"Huh?" She realized he'd asked her a question.

"So, does this sound like something you'd fund?"

She'd hardly heard a word he'd said. "I'd need to see a full proposal before I could say more."

"Yeah. Makes sense. Any suggestions for the format?"

"Tell you what. Bring your brother to my Wish Upon A Star workshop tomorrow night. We help people pin down their dreams."

"You hold a workshop on dreams?" He raised his eyebrows.

"You've heard of investment groups, haven't you? Networking groups? Often, people don't know what they want or are afraid to give voice to it. We brainstorm plans and offer mutual support to make dreams real."

"And what about the grants?"

"We provide a grant template and tips, too. But the purpose of the foundation is fulfilling dreams, not just giving away money. Let me show you."

She grabbed one of their new brochures from the end table and handed it to him. "Olivia Rasbergen's mission is to give money 'from the heart' to 'the little people.' We fund small businesses and services that deserve a chance, even if making a profit proves elusive."

"That fits Dale. He's not big on generating income."

"And that makes you angry?"

"No. Worried." Concern instantly replaced sarcasm. "He's stuck in limbo, kind of an eternal adolescence.

Ever since I dragged him to L.A. If I'd thought he'd drop out, I'd never have done it." Mitch shook his head. "So I feel responsible. If I can help him get his life straight, I want to do it."

"But is he happy with his life?"

Mitch shrugged. "He's got the rhetoric down, the old 'screw materialism and Yuppie striving.' He'd never tell me what he really thinks."

"Because you're his big brother."

"Exactly. We push each other's buttons. You know how it is." His hard eyes had softened as he talked about his brother, which made her like him a little more.

"I can imagine." She was an only child of a single mother, but she understood sibling dynamics from clients and friends. "So tell him about the workshop. If he's interested, confirm with my assistant tomorrow. You can pay the fee when you get there."

"There's a fee?"

"Nominal. Just a hundred dollars. That way participants make a real commitment to the process. That's why we offer matching grants, so they invest financially as well as emotionally and spiritually."

"You ask them for capital? Up front?"

"Investment signals action. We encourage them to find outside investors as well."

"I see." But the idea seemed to confirm some suspicion he had.

"We eventually want the foundation to be self-sustaining." Part of the long-range plan she had no clue how to create.

"If Dale does the workshop, will he get a grant?"

"If he meets our criteria. And if it's his dream. I had

a client today who thought she wanted a business, but what she wanted was to become a teacher."

"So you turned her down?"

"I shifted her focus. She's coming to the workshop and she'll probably change her application to a scholarship. Bring Dale and you'll see how it works." She touched his hand—a reassuring gesture she used all the time—but it was like a lightning rod for the sexual current between them. She jerked her hand away.

Mitch looked at his hand, then at her face, as if he'd felt the charge, too. When he spoke, he seemed groggy, like someone awakened from a stage hypnosis. "What are the, uh, criteria?"

She used words he would respect. "We have a rubric to evaluate the viability of the idea, the level of the applicant's commitment and the value of the service or product."

"That sounds good." He seemed relieved, which irked her.

"And, of course, I read the palm of every applicant."

"You what?"

"I'm teasing, but my gift helps me choose who to fund."

"Ok-ka-a-ay." He wanted to laugh, she could tell, and that irritated her. She usually avoided skeptics or ignored their insults, but Mitch got to her. Maybe because of her own recent doubts.

"If it makes you feel better, just call it my strong intuition and knowledge of human psychology."

"Fair enough," he said. "What's your approval percentage?"

"I've only been here for a few weeks, so I can't say. The first director funded a dozen projects and I—"

"What happened to the first director?"

"She had to leave because of a family illness."

"I see." Was he thinking she was a desperation hire? She'd feared that, too, though Olivia had said no. *You are tuned to the beat of every heart,* cara, *like I don't know what for,* she'd said in her charming Italian-cum-New Jersey accent. *I should have gone with my heart and hired you first. Forget my brothers and their obligations.*

"Anyway, I've funded six grants so far, including an earth-friendly organic bakery, a program for poor kids to earn computers through good grades and another to help prostitutes turn their lives around."

"Prostitutes?"

"Yes. It's a career-skills program. You can see how wide-ranging our projects can be."

"Is there a prospectus or annual report? I noticed you don't have a Web site."

"Just the brochure so far. Belinda, my assistant, is working on the Web site, which should be up soon. We're doing good work, Mitch, even if we don't have a paper trail."

"Sorry. I'm a lawyer. If it's not in triplicate with six signatures, it doesn't exist." He gave a self-mocking smile.

"Have a little faith."

"Not in my nature." He shrugged.

"That's not quite true." She'd caught flickers of a wistful optimism behind his judgmental eyes. His self-mocking humor spoke of the humility she'd remembered. "Who knows? Maybe you'll decide to draft your own grant."

"Why would you think that?"

"I sense some dissatisfaction in you."

"You're reading my mind?" He was teasing, but she answered him straight.

"Only dimly. When I know someone my gift fades." She had picked up a muddy blue coated with gray when she first saw him, signifying emotional reluctance, guardedness and suspicion. Not at all the openhearted guy she'd met that star-streaked night. But then maybe she'd read him wrong, read his palm wrong, too, as with her mother. That made her throb with pain. The day after she'd met Doctor X, her confidence, her world, had been rocked to its foundations.

She didn't need any gift to read Mitch's skepticism. "Everyone has psychic abilities, Mitch, however rudimentary or undeveloped. Even you. We all respond to subtle information about the people around us."

She watched him fight a sharp remark, then decide to keep the peace. "Maybe you're right."

"Come to the workshop with an open mind and you'll see."

"Okay," he said softly. "Surprise me."

He'd sure surprised her.

Why hadn't it been the friendly and familiar Jonathan smiling down at her when she'd shoved the eye bag off her face? Instead, it was Doctor X, who'd turned out all wrong.

The universe didn't give you what you wanted, she knew, it gave you what you needed.

She *needed* Mitch Margolin? A brusque and suspicious lawyer who thought she belonged in a rubber room? It seemed impossible. Despite that, even after he'd gone she was shaking with arousal.

If he came to the workshop tomorrow night, she

would get a chance to separate the tug of lust from the nudge of fate.

It just couldn't be him.

Could it?

A LITTLE PUNCHY from the encounter with Esmeralda, Mitch swung by his office to pick up some files and to see if Craig had returned his call. He had to verify that the foundation was sound now that he'd promised to bring Dale to her workshop.

On *dreams*. God Almighty, how had she talked him into that?

It was that husky voice, those eerie eyes. And that mouth...

"You again!" Maggie, his motherly secretary, looked at him with dismay. "When you left here at four, soldier, I thought you were finally acting like a civilian."

Maggie was always on him to take it easier. Her husband was retired military and Maggie swore that all the moves had taught her how to determine what mattered in life.

When you've packed as much as I have, you know what to U-Haul and what to yard-sale.

"Julie around?" he asked. He preferred to avoid her, at least until he got over the pain of his stupid crush. It had been three weeks, though. Should be time enough.

"Working at home." Maggie's steel-gray eyes were sympathetic. She'd figured it out, he guessed, and that made him feel even more ridiculous.

Before his crush on Julie had dead-ended, Maggie had strong-armed him into dating one of her daughter's single friends—a PR woman with her own firm, as driven as he was. He'd liked her a lot, but they eventually got tired of matching calendars. When he'd felt only relief, it dawned on him what had kept him so disengaged. Julie. The way he felt about her.

He liked to hit problems straight on, so he'd asked her out to dinner, aching to lay it on the line. The rub was that they worked together. Also, she was younger than him. But if she felt like he felt, they'd figure out a solution.

She'd wanted to talk to him, too, it turned out, which gave him hope. As soon as they took their first sip of the wine he'd selected in the restaurant he'd chosen for its romantic ambiance, reserving a private table, she'd told him how much his friendship meant and how grateful she was that he'd taken her on right out of law school, and she wanted him to be the first to know that she was *engaged to be married.*

To some bureaucrat in land management. Dull as the dirt he parceled.

Mitch should have spoken up sooner. Why had he waited? Too late then and his confession had died in his chest. He'd wished her well. Of course. He wanted her to be happy.

He'd just hoped it would be with him.

"Dinner's in your office," Maggie said now. "A basket of homemade tamales from the wife of the landscape guy to thank you for all the extras. I could buy a new house with the billables you give away, Mitchell. Keep it up and your pro bonos will make us pro-broke-os."

"I see their tax statements, Maggie. It does not serve us well to break their piggy banks paying us." His clients often needed piddly advice he could rattle off without any research. "It's practice-building," he said. "Gets me referrals."

Maggie rolled her eyes. He was swamped and she knew it.

The way he saw it was you gave extra and extra came back to you. Esmeralda would call it karma. He called it good business.

Right out of school, he'd gotten tons of experience with a business-law firm. Pro-bono work with the Small Business Administration helping startups had fired his blood, so he'd opened his own firm with that specialty six years ago, hired Maggie, then grew enough to bring on Julie last year.

He was up to his eyeballs in work, but he'd begun to feel restless, as though he needed a new challenge. Craig was after him to work for the A.G.'s office. A big income dive, but it was important work. A good next step, he figured.

"Let me see if any of this is urgent." Maggie flipped through the pink message slips. "It can all wait. Go *home.*"

"When I'm ready. What are you doing here so late?"

"Keeping your head above water. Ed can heat up leftovers and Rachel's working. Soon enough I'll have more time than I'll know what to do with." She sighed and he realized she was talking about the fact that her daughter started college soon.

"You need time off to drive her up there?" She'd be attending Northern Arizona University in Flagstaff, just three hours away.

"Nope. Saturday's move-in day, so we'll drive up then."

"So hang with her a couple of days maybe."

"And be accused of clinging? She'd be mortified. No. We'll be fine. I'm just…antsy, I guess."

"You know what I'm going to say…."

"I don't need more school."

"A paralegal would really help. I'd pay your tuition."

"You don't need to do that," she said.

"It's a write-off. Good for my taxes."

"You are such a softie."

"Eh-eh-eh. I'm a ruthless shark and don't you forget it." He gave her a stern look. "If my clients hear otherwise, they'll quit me cold."

She smiled. "I'll take off then. Just don't stay too late." She shut down her computer, then adjusted the small photo of her daughter as a young girl, running a thumb across the surface in a sad and tender gesture.

Damn. He hated to see her blue. She had to stay busy. That was the secret. He'd cook up an extra assignment for her. *Hell.*

"What's that?" Maggie nodded at the brochure in his hand.

He looked down at it. "A foundation that offers grants. Something I'm looking into for Dale."

She leveled her gaze. "You can't live his life for him."

"Just a jumpstart, that's all. Craig call?"

"Nope. Sorry."

"I'll try him again."

"Don't stay—"

"Late, got it. Good night, *Mom.*"

"I don't know why I bother. You never listen to me." She was shaking her head as she walked out the door and he headed into his office. Maybe if he kept her busy nagging him, she wouldn't have time to miss her daughter.

Craig picked up on the first ring. "Craig Baker."

"I have you live?" They often traded voice mail for days just booking a racquetball game.

"Trying to catch up." Craig sighed. His friend was hopelessly overworked, which would be Mitch's fate if he came on board. Sounded good to him. He needed... something.

"I hate to bug you, but did you get a chance to look into that foundation?" Mitch dropped into his chair and rolled close to the desk, laying the purple brochure beside his keyboard.

"Not yet." Craig sighed. "I'm up to my ears. On top of everything else, there's media interest in the roofing company fraud case out in Sun City West. I'm prepping the press secretary."

An assistant A.G., Craig was part of a cross-agency task force to stem the tide of scam artists preying on Arizona's retirees. "I'll squeeze it in when I can."

"If it helps, I went there and met the director. I got a brochure if you want the names of board members and staff."

"Good idea. Give 'em to me." There was a rustle as he prepared to take notes.

Mitch read off the list. Craig stopped him halfway through. "Sylvestri? That name's familiar."

"Yep. There are two Sylvestris on the board. Enzo and Louis."

"Interesting. I'll get a secretary to run a Lexis-Nexis search and get back to you." That would provide any news mentions or lawsuits, at least. A place to start. "How did it seem when you were there?"

"Hard to tell. Quirky." Talk about understatement. "They have the grantees match funds and get investors."

"Ah…possible prepayment scam. That's how that MedQuest real estate investment group operated."

"Made me wonder, too." The phony music deal had been that kind of rip-off. A common music industry con, he'd learned afterward and was grateful they'd only lost a grand in "advance costs." He'd been young, of course, and con artists were clever. One of his clients, a savvy guy, recently lost his shirt to a group that funded invention prototypes. They left the country with his and a hundred other dreamers' "patent-filing fee."

"Also, the director is new. She replaced a woman who left supposedly because of a family illness."

"Major changes in top staff—especially early on—is a sign of trouble," Craig said, confirming his suspicion.

"Yeah." What would Craig say if he knew that Esmeralda got the job because she read palms? *Lord.*

"Got the name of the previous director?"

"I'll ask when I see the new one tomorrow night."

"You're seeing her again?" Craig perked up.

"She's holding a workshop for people looking at grants. I'm bringing Dale." He paused. "Funny thing is that I know her. I met her back when I had a band."

"So she was, what, a groupie?"

"Hardly." She'd liked when he'd played for her, though. Of course she'd had those incredible eyes and that great mouth….

"But you slept with her."

"Nah. She was jailbait." She'd seemed younger than she was—eighteen—and probably a virgin, and he'd been leaving for L.A. anyway….

"You were a *gentleman?* No wonder your band never made it."

"Yeah. That was the problem." *You will succeed beyond your wildest dreams,* she'd said, looking up from his palm. And he'd believed her. He couldn't imagine he'd ever been that naive. If he'd used the brains God gave him he'd have checked out the "scout" before leaving town.

"See what you can find out at the workshop," Craig said. "If it's bogus, you're doing a public service. You'll look good around here, too, if you're still interested in a job."

"I am." The idea got his blood pumping like when he'd first opened his practice. Something new. Something important.

They finished the call with a date for racquetball, which lately had been his main social outlet, along with tossing back some brews watching sports on TV with a few friends.

He liked long hours in the office, despite Maggie's nagging at him. It got too quiet at his house when Dale was out. Besides, he loved what he did. No regrets. Esmeralda had acted as if quitting music had been some kind of crime against humanity.

She'd looked at him so strangely, as though he was the ghost of Christmas past or a relative she'd thought lost at sea.

To be honest, he'd felt an odd vibration, too. Probably just sexual chemistry. Or maybe inhaling all that incense.

What had she told him? Scientific studies on palmar derma-whatever? Please. Psychics and palm readers were such common scammers, they'd practically earned their own fraud division.

Mitch didn't believe anyone's future rested in the lines of a palm. Now, fingerprints, on the other hand, those definitely said something about your future. For Dale's sake, he hoped Craig didn't find Esmeralda's anywhere.

3

AT HOME, MITCH FOUND HIS BROTHER on the couch, clutching a bowl of Cap'n Crunch with a big glop of peanut butter on top. Stoned again. Dale mainlined junk food whenever he fired up a bowl.

Dale looked up from the MTV reality show he was watching. "You're early." He shoved magazines and a Xbox controller to the floor and patted the cushion for Mitch. His gaze returned to the plasma screen.

Mitch grabbed the remote and thumbed down the sound. He would be casual. Start real easy, no pressure. "So, I stopped by that foundation office—the one you cut out from the paper?"

Slowly, Dale turned away from the screen. "What?"

"The place that gives grants? You wrote down that after-school music program idea? Wholesale instruments, remember?"

"Oh, yeah." He shrugged. No big deal. That was how he'd acted when the music store had failed. Dale treated job ideas like catch-and-release fishing. There would always be another one. Not so, Mitch knew. Some chances didn't come twice.

"So I found out more information for you."

"You didn't need to, but thanks." Dale was an easy-going guy, popular, with lots of women around. Always out and about, distracted from any doubts he had about the way he lived.

Maybe Mitch should have done the tough-love thing and booted him out, but he couldn't stand the idea of his brother dragging his cookbooks and guitar from friend's sofa to friend's sofa. Mitch had the room and the money to help, so he did.

"The grant sounds possible. We need a proposal, though, and here's the deal—there's a grant-writing workshop tomorrow we need to go to. They'll give tips." *And maybe hold a séance? God.*

"Tomorrow night? We've got a gig."

"This is at seven. And it's a foot in the door on the grant."

Dale chewed thoughtfully. "How about if you just cover it for me?" He turned to the TV. "I've got a couple of lessons in the late afternoon."

"So skip your nap. Come on. This could be great." He kept himself from saying anything harsh or pushy. *Easy does it.*

"It was just an idea, Mitch. No big thing."

"It was a good idea. Give yourself some credit."

"I don't know." He shrugged, but Mitch knew he was just afraid of trying something new. Dale's band sold a decent number of downloads off MySpace, but it wasn't enough to make a living, to be independent, to build up any security.

"The director was encouraging. And you're good with your students. Working with kids would be great for you."

Nothing.

"Make an effort here." He took a weary breath.

"I'm getting on your nerves, living here so long, huh? I can stay at Bailey's or with Sarah."

"No. I'm glad you're here. I have the space." And, frankly, he enjoyed the company. "I just want you to—"

"Become you. Yeah, I get that. I don't intend to bust my hump six days a week like you."

"There's nothing wrong with my life." He had rewarding work, friends, a nice home, money in the bank.

"You need to get laid, bro," Dale said. "You're a lot easier to get along with when you're gettin' it regular."

Mitch rolled his eyes.

"You don't even play anymore. Hell, you used to write."

"Not interested," Mitch said. He hadn't even thought about music in years. His guitar was in his closet, way out of tune. Music used to be everything to him— making it, listening to it, analyzing it—but that came from being young and ambitious and obsessed with making a mark.

"I'm getting on your nerves. I should move out."

"Stay. For God's sake, I'm just trying to—"

"You're mad that I trashed the kitchen making that reduction?"

"Not at all." Dale aspired to be a gourmet cook, except he preferred improvising to following recipes. Which worked fine in music, not so fine in the kitchen. "Maybe less salt next time." He'd choked down some of the glop to be polite. "Meet me at the workshop, would you?"

"You're not gonna let up? I'll try to be there. You hungry? I've got vegan chili in the slow cooker."

"Sure." What could Dale do to chili, after all? Mitch followed his brother into the kitchen, which looked like a food bomb had gone off, scattering chunks of onion, garlic cloves, spices and pinto beans everywhere. The counter was littered with grocery bags and Dale's exotic cookbooks—he had an entire book for braising, one for cooking chiles, another for Mongolian fare.

Dale flipped on some music and Mitch recognized the Xtent of the Crime demo the band had cut. "What made you play that?"

Dale shrugged. "A little voice in my head." He grinned the grin that made him look like a kid again. He was as sunny as Esmeralda. She had a purpose, at least, kooky as it was. Dale bounced around, did whatever felt good.

He'd stayed in L.A. for six years after the band had broken up, surviving on studio work and band hookups, until he'd come home dead broke. How could he be so aimless?

It made Mitch nuts. Life was more than just getting through the days undamaged. You had to grow, accomplish things, make a difference.

"Wait'll you taste this." Dale scooped chili into two bowls. It smelled good, at least.

"Not too much for me." If it was terrible, he could nibble, then dump it when Dale wasn't looking.

The next song came on, and he realized he'd sung this one to Esmeralda that night. He'd only written a couple of ballads—thank God, since the overwrought lyrics made him cringe. She'd sighed with pleasure, making him want to roll her onto the grass and never stop kissing her sweet mouth.

He noticed a grocery sack from the nearby Chinese market. Beside it, a wire mesh bowl held fruit—small, bright-red strawberries, a couple of kiwis, a clump of what looked like pale, oversized raspberries. He picked one up. "What's this?"

"That's a lychee," Dale said. "Put out the rest."

In the sack he found more kiwi and several yellow, grooved fruit the size of small apples that he recognized. "Star fruit?"

Dale shot him a look, surprised he knew. "Yeah."

"A friend of mine likes these." He sniffed the cool surface. Pears. *Yeah.* And Esmeralda's mouth. *Mmm.* He was getting moony over a piece of fruit and a pair of turquoise eyes.

And a mouth. Don't forget the mouth....

Dale handed him a bowl and a spoon.

Maybe if Dale knew about Esmeralda, he'd be more interested. "Remember the girl I met at that fair we played before we went to L.A.?"

"That chick you were sitting on the hill with all night?"

"That's the one."

"She was hot."

"That's who runs the foundation. And the workshop."

"You're kidding. Small world, huh?"

"Yeah." Esmeralda seemed to think their meeting had cosmic significance. Good Lord. She made him... nervous. One minute she made sense, the next she said something loony, then she joked—

"So you like the chili, I guess."

He stopped, the spoon near his mouth. Thinking of Esmeralda, he'd mindlessly sucked down half the bowl. He paused to actually taste it. *Blech.* Grainy and dry and bitter with garlic. "You're getting there," he said, trying not to gag. "So you can meet her tomorrow night?"

Dale shrugged.

"Save me a few of these," Mitch said, tapping a star fruit. He would take them as a peace offering. Go early and offer to help. Say nothing to offend her. Kook or not, she was in charge of a million-dollar foundation and could be Dale's ticket out of limbo. He'd give her the benefit of the doubt. At least until he heard from Craig.

THE NEXT DAY, ESMERALDA GRABBED her yogurt from the office kitchen and headed to the front desk to check the afternoon schedule. Belinda should be at lunch, but she was hunched over a palmistry book, chewing a nail.

"Belinda?"

She jerked up. "Oh, Esmeralda. Sorry. I'm studying. It's my lunch break, though, so I'm not robbing the foundation."

"It's fine. I just wanted to check the schedule."

"I booked you back-to-back till five. Is that okay? Or do you want an hour in there to work on proposals? You know, I could save you time by prescreening some grants if you—"

"The schedule's fine, Belinda. And you should take a lunch break. Eat something."

"I'm fine. I want to be available. You never know when you-know-who might call." She grinned. "Oh, that reminds me." She read from a message slip. "A Mitch Margolin called to say he and his brother will attend the workshop tonight. Make sense?"

"Yes. Thank you." *He might be the one.* Belinda would be thrilled to hear that, but Esmeralda wasn't ready to accept it herself yet.

"So, how's it going?" Esmeralda nodded at the palmistry book and sat beside Belinda, dipping into her yogurt.

"Not so hot." Belinda sighed. "I can't get the fingers—shape and lines and color. Last night, I was looking at this woman's Mercury finger, and I thought it was long, but then it shrank before my eyes, so I couldn't tell. I just froze."

"Trust your first impulse," she said. Belinda had the same enthusiasm Esmie had had when she'd started, but nowhere near the confidence. But then Esmie had sometimes been too sure of herself at first.

"Let me show you a couple of things." She found the finger diagram in the book and talked through a few examples.

"I get it now," Belinda said. "You make it so easy. This is fun, isn't it? Talking like this."

"Sure. It's great." Especially when she could see Belinda making progress.

"This is embarrassing, but sometimes I feel like you're, like, my big sister, you know? I got so sick of three brothers."

"I'm honored," she said, very touched by the affection.

"I want you to know how much I appreciate everything. You're so patient and I can be such a blockhead. Did you see I got you that new tea?"

"I did. You don't need to do extras. I can wash my car when it needs it. Really."

"I know, but I know Olivia made you hire me. I just want you to be glad you have me."

"I am glad. Very." Olivia had asked her to take Belinda under her wing and she was happy to. Belinda was smart and had potential if she could just lower her anxiety level.

Belinda was eyeing her yogurt.

"Here. Finish it." She held it out.

"I can't take your lunch."

"I'm full. Also, there's some teriyaki tofu in the fridge if you're still hungry."

"Are you sure? I really, really appreciate it."

"It's nothing. Enjoy. So, how's the ledger coming? Rico helping you get it down?"

"Yes. Slowly. It's coming. I'll have what you need by the board meeting." She bit her lip. "There's one thing. Rico wanted me to ask you about a grant that an associate of his applied for. It's a company that holds charity auctions of teddy bears dressed up like famous people. Corporations sponsor the bears that then get donated to crisis nurseries. It's very cool."

"I don't recall."

"You probably didn't get to it yet. I know you're behind. That's why I offered to help." She looked at her. "But if you don't think I'm ready..."

"Give me this week, Belinda, to get a feel for the system, then maybe I can hand off some of it to you."

"Okay." She thought that over. "Anyway, Rico was wondering if you could put a rush on it? Uncle Louis knows the guy, so Aunt Olivia would want to fund it and all."

"I'll let you know."

"Okay. I told him I'd ask. Anyway, do you need anything for the workshop tonight? You've got newsprint, easels, markers?"

"I've got everything I need," she said. *Including the man from her past.* Which gave her mixed feelings. The only thing they had in common was a hot-asblazes attraction, and you could hardly build a future on *that*. She needed some kind of sign, an assurance. Some proof...

She noticed the newspaper folded to the horoscopes page.

"Want to check yours?" Belinda handed it to her.

Newspaper horoscopes were far too general to be meaningful, but on the cover was a photo of a starry sky with the headline, First Of Falling Stars To Light August Skies. She read on. The Pleiades meteor shower was scheduled to begin tonight. The same astronomical wonder that had lit the sky the night she'd met Doctor X.

Maybe this was the sign. Mitch could stay after the workshop and they would watch the stars shoot across the sky and he would feel like Doctor X again. And she would know it was right.

"Esmeralda? Is it something bad in your stars?"

"I hope not," she said softly. "I hope it's something really, really good."

A HALF-HOUR BEFORE the Wish Upon A Star Workshop, Esmeralda checked the mirror. The spaghetti-strapped black silk tank top looked nice with the turquoise-and-yellow silk skirt. The colors would stimulate creativity and calm, she thought, and she liked the way the handkerchief hem tickled her calves.

She'd struggled to get ready, what with all the phone calls she'd juggled. Nail clients and palm clients and friends wanting appointments and advice and attaboys. Also her neighbor, Jimbo, needed her car again. He was a mechanic who kept her Jetta in tip-top shape, but kept giving away his own cars.

She was mostly ready for the workshop. Just a little more fussing with the food, arranging the furniture, setting up the computer display.

The doorbell rang. Someone was way early.

Her two foster dogs set up a racket and raced her to the door. Huffington, a spindly-legged bulldog, was an old soul, whose rheumy eyes declared he knew it all and had done it twice. Pistol, a wild-eyed cairn terrier, lived to snitch food and knew how to fetch, dance and shake hands. They'd been with her for a month and every day they stayed made it harder to let them go.

That was the worst thing about being a foster owner. How did her friend who ran the rescue shelter handle the repeated losses? Esmeralda tried to stay light in life, to accept hellos and good-byes with an even response, but this was murder.

Sonny and Cher, the two cats lurking on the ledge above the living room, were brother and sister calicos scheduled to go to new homes in a few days. She'd only had them a week, so it wouldn't be such agony when they left.

She hushed the dogs and went to the door, startled to find Mitch on her porch holding a paper sack. He looked great in a purple silk shirt and black cargo pants.

Her heart pounded so hard she held her chest when she opened the door.

Mitch entered and their gazes locked for a startling moment of intensity and recognition, almost relief. Unmistakably powerful, and it gave her hope. "I'm glad you came," she said, the pulse of pleasure in her body making her wobbly.

"I'm glad, too," he said. He seemed surprised that he'd said that and, maybe, that it was true.

She became aware that the dogs were going nuts, jumping up on Mitch. "I'm sorry," she said, crouching to grab their collars. "Down, guys." She fought her own leaping emotions.

"It's okay." Mitch squatted with her. "Who are these guys?"

She told him.

"Great names."

"I didn't pick them. They're foster pets. The cats, too." She pointed up at the ledge where the cats stared down at them.

"Foster pets, huh?" he said, ruffling Huffington's fur.

"My friend Jill has a rescue shelter, but she ran out of space. So they're with me until she finds them homes."

"That's generous of you."

"Who could resist these guys?" She rested her cheek against Huffington's neck, feeling Mitch's eyes on her.

"I can see that." He had to clear his throat. "Anyway, Dale's supposed to stop by for a while. He's got a gig, so I'm the designated note-taker."

"It's nice of you to help him out," she said.

"It's my only hope of getting him off my couch." But she sensed the tenderness behind the sarcasm.

"What's in the sack?" she asked.

"A thank you." He handed it to her.

Inside the bag she found three star fruit. "How did you know? This is what's missing from my fruit tray. My store was out."

"The Asian market near my house always has exotic stuff."

She sniffed one of the smooth, cool fruits. "Mmm."

"Smells like pears?" he asked.

"Yeah." She held it out, fingers trembling, and he bent to sniff, his dark eyes searching hers out, sexual sparks lighting their depths.

"Reminds me of that night," he said softly.

"I know." And the star shower would add to the memory. She wanted to kiss him now, just to see if it would feel the same. Was this their moment? Did he feel it, too?

"Can I help you?"

"Help me?" *Yes, yes, oh, yes.* She was lost in her fantasy.

He grinned. "Cut up the fruit? For the workshop? Hello?"

She gathered herself. "Oh. Yes. That would be great. Let me put the dogs away."

He helped her up from the floor, as he'd done the afternoon before. She liked his firm grip, the way he took charge. Their eyes met again. She wished suddenly the workshop was over and they could go out back and watch the stars fly and she could tell him about the prediction and—

The man would run for the hills. He already thought she was a borderline kook. *Slow down. Let things unfold as they will.*

When she returned to the living room after putting the dogs away, Mitch was watching her. He seemed to have to drag his eyes away to look around the room. "You expecting a crowd?" He meant the extra chairs, loveseat, end tables and sofa.

"Just fifteen people. The extra furniture belongs to a friend. I'm keeping it until she's sure living with her boyfriend will work out."

"You're a soft touch."

"She's a friend." She shrugged. The Early American stuff clashed mightily with the simple designs and the magenta, lime and orange colors of the Pier 1 Imports decor Esmeralda had chosen.

"The extra art is hers?" He meant the framed pieces of art braced against all the walls.

"No. That's my roommate's. Annika Morris. She's an art therapist." Esmie had hung as many pieces as would fit among her own framed photos and the map collages she'd made with Jonathan. "She's just here until her grant comes through or she gets a job. She'll be at the workshop tonight."

"You've got a lot going on. Roommates, foster pets, furniture storage, a new job—"

The phone rang, proving his point.

"I like to keep busy," she said, rushing to answer it. It was Jill confirming the cats' pick-up.

"Not a lot of peace and quiet, I take it," he said when Esmie hung up.

"I do fine." But coming home to a dozen phone messages every night had lately been wearying. Probably just adjusting to the new job. The phone rang again. "Excuse me?" That one was a friend needing advice. She made a lunch date for a more in-depth conversation.

He gave her a look.

"What? So maybe it's a little hectic at times."

"That's what phone machines are for. People take advantage if you let them."

"The more you give, the more you have to give."

"Some people take until you say no."

"That's quite the world view you have. I don't know how I'd get up in the morning feeling that negative."

"It's not negative. It's realistic. If you accept human nature, you don't have misunderstandings and you don't get disappointed."

"Or you expect the best and people strive to meet your expectations."

"I think I read that on the wall of your office."

He made her idealism seem silly. She rarely had to defend herself, since everyone she knew respected her abilities. This man was like a blast of cold water in the middle of a hot shower. "I happen to believe it's true."

"I guess we see things differently." The pity and judgment in his expression were like a brand on her skin.

"But you know you're right, don't you?" She was startled by how quickly her response to him had changed. She went from attraction to hope to irritation to anger with lightning speed.

"No more than you do."

"You think that by helping others I neglect myself and what I really want? Is that what you think?"

He shrugged.

"I can assure you that's not what's happening." She hated how defensive she sounded. She was usually calm and patient and balanced in her remarks.

"You would be in a position to know."

"And I do know," she snapped, then caught herself. "Why am I arguing with you?" She sagged, frustrated and upset and so maddeningly hot for the man.

"I don't know. Frankly, I'm in no position to criticize. My sofa's got a permanent sag from my brother sleeping there, my remote is stained orange from his Cheetos, and I'm here doing his homework."

She laughed lightly. "So, you're a soft touch, too?"

"Just ask my secretary."

"I don't know why I'm so defensive," she said. "Maybe it's because I know you don't approve of me."

"Maybe I just don't understand you." He was being kind.

She appreciated the gesture, but couldn't quite let it stand. "And what you do understand, you disagree with."

"Not...exactly." He rolled his shoulder. "We've got détente. Let's leave it at that, why don't we?"

"You're right. After you cut up the star fruit, maybe you can help me arrange the furniture?" And during the meteor shower, maybe he'd sense their cosmic bond and they could get past butting heads.

Right, and maybe Huffington and Pistol would do a minuet on the kitchen table.

4

IN THE KITCHEN, ESMIE WATCHED Mitch stop dead at the display of fruit tarts, chocolate-covered strawberries, frosted brownies and the fruit tray she'd prepared. She'd also set out plastic champagne flutes and was icing several inexpensive bottles.

"Wow. You went all out."

"Except for the star fruit. See how it's missing?" She indicated the tray of raspberries, blueberries, kiwi, lychee and persimmon, where the horseshoe design left an obvious spot for the missing fruit. Stars had always been significant in her life, and she incorporated the image wherever she could. She'd have mentioned that to anyone but Mitch, who, at best, would give her the indulgent smile reserved for a child who'd heard reindeer on the roof on Christmas Eve.

She frowned at the thought, handing him a paring knife. When he took it, their fingers met and heat shot through her. She lifted her gaze to his. Light glinted off the knife blade and made her blink. Or maybe it was the glare from his glasses.

Something made her knees go weak. Wasn't there something about friction making sex hotter? Sounded like a *Cosmo* tip, not something Esmeralda believed.

She wanted sexual feelings to be comfortable and easy, not jagged and unsettling and a little bit rough.

"How do you want it?" he asked softly.

Anyway you give it.

"Thin or thick or in between," he added.

It all sounds good. She caught herself, realizing he meant the fruit, though his tone had simmered with heat. "Whichever." She swayed, off balance, and bumped the tray with her hip, jarring it forward.

"Easy there." He set down the knife and steadied her by her arms, his fingers covering her straps. "You've got to do something about these." He lifted them, one at a time, back in place, running a slow finger over each one.

"When I move, they slip," she breathed.

"And you move a lot. You're very…wiggly."

"You think so?"

He nodded slowly.

She became aware of that tightness between her legs and a swooshing feeling inside, like a wind that could lift her off her feet.

Mitch released her, but his eyes held hers, studying them closely. "You have incredible eyes. I never forgot them."

They were her most powerful feature, she knew. Their color churned from jade to turquoise to crystal blue and back in a way that made people stare. Turquoise signified psychic ability, of course, but her mother believed Esmie's irises revealed she had a rich soul.

"I remember yours, too." White-hot points of desire gleamed from the center of each dark marble at the moment.

"Just an ordinary brown."

"Not ordinary at all." She felt tugged in, pulled to him.

The moment stretched, they leaned closer until Mitch's hip bumped the tray, which brought them both back to what they were doing.

"I'd better get cutting." Mitch grabbed the knife and sliced the first fruit open, baring its juicy yellow center. The air filled with that sweet smell that took her back to the night they'd kissed, fruit juice on their lips.

The *click-snick* of Mitch's knife teased her ears and she was entranced by his deft movements. What great fingers he had. Jupiter…Saturn…Apollo…Mercury…all working together in perfect rhythm. Strong and long, with the square tips of an analytical person. How would they be on her body? Probing, seeking, sure of what they wanted, giving pleasure with every slide and twist and stroke and rub….

Stop that. The fingers were more than just sexual tools. They were predictors of a person's strengths and challenges.

Noticing her stare, he stopped cutting. "Too thick?"

"No, no. I was just studying your fingers. They're nice."

He held up his hand, wiggled the digits, shiny with juice, then shrugged. "Look normal to me."

"Finger shape and angle reflect personality," she said, deciding to share some knowledge. "For example, you have smooth knuckles." She lightly skimmed the backs of his fingers. "That signifies leadership ability."

"Oh, yeah?" His gaze flickered at the contact.

"Yes. And your fingers have a lateral curve, especially Jupiter—the index finger—which means you're a serious person who guards his emotions."

"Ok-k-kay." His skepticism seemed to be competing with how much he liked her hands on him.

"That's also indicated by your long Saturn finger—" she touched his middle finger "—which shows a strong sense of duty and responsibility." Her voice had gone shaky. "The square fingertips show an analytical nature."

"If you say so." He cleared his throat again, not being analytical at all at the moment.

She imagined lifting this juice-sweet hand to her breast and melting against him. Her sex was a throbbing pulse.

He took her hand and looked it over, running his fingers along its edge. "Your fingers curve, but you're not guarded."

"It's not the same kind of curve. My hands are different."

"They're smaller...and softer," he said, looking up at her, still holding her hand, sending electricity flying between them.

She shivered and her strap slipped again.

"Allow me." With his free hand, Mitch slowly dragged it into place, leaving a moist trail of juice on her arm.

"Thank you," she breathed.

"My pleasure." He wiped the moisture from her skin, still holding her gaze.

This was ridiculous. They were holding hands, fondling straps, wiping up juice and staring at each other. She had to get this under control for now. For later, well, they'd see.

"The furniture," she blurted.

"Excuse me?"

"Let's finish with this and move the furniture, huh?" She pulled her hand away, grabbed the stars he'd cut and turned to arrange them on the tray, grateful when Mitch's knife began clicking away again.

She hoped the big-muscle work of shifting sofas would ease the tension, but she couldn't clear her head of his scent or her nerves from continual pulses of arousal, which got worse every time they brushed arms and bumped hips as they maneuvered tables and chairs into place.

Mitch seemed to be constantly dragging his gaze from her body, and he did a lot of throat-clearing. It was as though they were being swirled down the drain of an irresistible attraction, while they clung to the slick, sloped sides of the tub. Whether it was ordinary lust or cosmic forces, she couldn't yet tell.

Mitch moved the Early American sofa where she asked, treating the monstrous thing as though it was made of balsa wood. He was so deliciously strong. He rose, not even breathing hard from the effort. "Anything else you need from me?"

A million things and they all started with his mouth. And his fingers. And that broad back. "Uh, maybe put the newsprint pads on easels?" They were for small-group time when participants brainstormed solutions to each other's problems.

While he did that, she set up the computer for the presentation on the grant template.

"Exactly what's going to happen here tonight?" Mitch asked when he'd finished.

Stay for the meteor shower and you'll see. She explained the networking, grant-writing tips, brainstorming and goal-setting portions of the workshop.

"Sounds reasonable." He acted as though he'd

expected something bizarre or laughable. So of course she had to startle him.

"And then we strip and dance naked in a circle under the moon, chanting Druid spells."

His eyebrows shot up as she'd expected.

"I'm joking." She paused. "But there's a spiritual aspect to it, too. The idea is to verbalize what you want, write it down, put energy behind it and attract success. This approach works. It's been documented."

She watched him fight his skepticism to smile. "Hell, if it would get my brother into something good, I'd strip naked and dance under the moon myself."

"That I'd love to see." Her words held surprising heat. Not how she usually flirted. Around Mitch she felt raw and hungry, not light and easy as she usually felt when she anticipated going to bed with someone.

She enjoyed sex—the warmth, the connection, the wonder of two bodies moving together in pleasure. For those moments, she felt part of the life force, eternal and timeless.

But sex with Mitch would be different. It would be intense, erotic and a little scary, like daring yourself to look down from the top of a forty-story building.

She'd sensed that when they'd kissed all those years ago. She'd been a virgin—technically—but she'd made out plenty. Never until that night had she felt a need so ferocious it made her liquid with desire. And here it was again. Only this time she knew exactly what to do about it.

"I almost wish I were psychic," Mitch said. "I'd love to read your mind right now."

"I think you already are."

"Ah." He shifted closer, his dark eyes intense, then retreated. The electric tug between them seemed to trouble him, too. "So you just write down a wish and it comes true. Like 'I want to become an astronaut or a ballet dancer or—'"

"A rock star?" She'd meant to tease, but his embarrassed expression made her instantly sorry.

"Yeah. That." He grinned, but she'd sensed his pain. *He'd believed her prediction and it had been wrong.*

The truth was ice water down her back. She'd failed him as she'd failed her mother. And he'd been hurt. "I'm so sorry. When I predicted your success, I was just learning and I—"

"Forget it. You told me to go for it. Big deal. I was a kid. We both were."

"But I—"

"You told me what I wanted to hear, Esmeralda. That was years ago. Forget it."

The doorbell rang. She stood there, wanting to tell him her mistake was a learner's arrogance, that she'd become better. But what if her mistake had led to the cynicism she saw in him now?

"Get the door. It's show time." He smiled at her, his face full of kind sympathy. "Relax. We'll talk after. I'll help you put back that monster sofa."

"All right." Mitch was staying and her every chakra pulsed with energy. She'd never felt so alive around a man.

She headed for the door, troubled by the quicksilver of her emotions around him. Everything changeable, everything intense. If they were meant for each other, she would never have a moment's peace or harmony. How could that be right?

MITCH PASSED THE BOX OF chocolates shaped like geni-
talia to his left, mortified as hell. He didn't dare make
eye contact with a soul now that they were nibbling
boobs or cocks in dark, milk or white chocolate. Good
Lord. Esmeralda hadn't mentioned people would be
bringing *samples*, but apparently the sex candy woman
wanted to create a mail-order business.

The workshop wasn't turning out to be as sensible as
Esmeralda had made it sound. There were a few grant-
writing tips, sure, and he'd taken notes, but mostly it was
pep squad rah-rah and mystical bullshit.

Three of the participants were outright nut cases, a
couple were borderline criminals and the kindest thing
he could say about the rest was they were…quirky.
Well, that girl and her father with the kiddie gym idea
were normal enough, if the dad would just quit trying
to live through the daughter and let her get a teaching
degree. *Sheesh.* He could hire a manager if he didn't
want to run the gym himself.

Right before the candy lady did her thing, a woman
had passed out samples of customized sexy lingerie,
saying something about regular women looking ridiculous in the off-the-rack stuff. As she pointed out
the features of each item, Mitch kept picturing Esmeralda wearing it. He could imagine her sweet nipples
through that lacy slip thing, envision her shapely legs
snug in those red fishnets, see her breasts swell above
a black half bra.

He shifted his legs to be sure his erection didn't show.
Around her, his lust hit with an unexpected wallop, like
some frou-frou drink made with six hard liquors. It

mowed him flat. Well, all except the part that stood straight up. *Damn.*

Now and then her sizzling eyes would catch his. She wanted something from him. Something big. Which made him conclude he would help her with her furniture, but not with those wiggly straps. No way. Talk about asking for trouble.

He had the grant to work out, and he wasn't up for dealing with her strange and silly beliefs. She treated the kooks and crooks with the same respect she gave the sensible people.

Take the guy who owned a girlie bar and wanted to do something "plaque-worthy" for his strippers. A muscle-bound bartender who worked at his club was looking to be an investment banker. Yeah, right.

Dale never showed. Which irritated Mitch, but he'd taken good notes, ignoring the goofball stuff about positive visualizations and universal energy. He'd talk it up to Dale, tread lightly, ease him on board.

He was relieved when Esmeralda announced the workshop was over. She had everyone recite affirmations to each other. The room echoed with Gregorian chants of wishful thinking: *I can see my dream and make it happen…. I am smart and capable and savvy…. I know what I want and how to get it…. I am a successful writer…artist…entrepreneur…*

Whatever. He tried not to roll his eyes or laugh. The sad part was that with her wide-eyed optimism and naiveté, Esmeralda would have a hard time saying no to the bad ideas.

On the other hand, Dale's project should be a slam dunk. Not only was it a practical endeavor, but it also had tangible, measurable results.

Unless the foundation was bogus. He hoped Craig had news for him tomorrow.

Esmeralda walked everyone to the door, then closed it and turned to Mitch. They were alone and it was very quiet. Time to put back the furniture then take off.

"So, what did you think?" Esmeralda asked, her eyes bright, digging at him.

"It was…interesting," he said, not wanting to offend her. "I took a lot of notes on the grant for Dale."

"You didn't like it?"

"It's just that…some of those people were…out there. I mean the guy with the strip club?"

"Duke? I think it's a great idea to offer financial coaching to his employees. The strippers tend to waste all the cash they earn."

"What about that 'misunderstanding with the law' he was talking about?"

"I think it was just a PR problem."

"What about the muscle-bound guy who wants to be a stock broker?"

"Jasper? We're working on his gambling problem. Duke's workshop is a great first step."

"He'd be better off if you just told him no, right out. Who takes stock tips from a bouncer who belongs to Gamblers Anonymous?"

"He deserves a chance, Mitch. He knows he has a problem and that's the first step."

"Some people are crazy or crooks," he said.

"Everyone here was sincere. Surely you could see that."

"Sincerity is coin of the realm for con artists. That's their pathology and why they're so successful. And as for crazy…? I don't think you want to be giving grants to unstable people."

"I know how to read people."

She was blindly optimistic and it made him want to shake her awake. "I hope you're not talking about your psychic powers?"

She sucked in a breath.

"That came out badly." He didn't want to start an argument. "I just mean you have to be careful, use good judgment. I don't mean to tell you what to do—"

"But you are. I guess your training makes you assume the worst about people."

"I don't assume the worst. I understand human nature."

She looked at him with a mix of pity and exasperation. "Let me explain it to you. The foundation is about letting people spread their wings, take chances. Think about Annika's project—art therapy for troubled kids. That could sound frivolous to some foundations, especially those who deal with survival issues. But that's our niche, that's where we fit."

"So, has she got a grant for sure?" Mitch asked, hoping to pin down Dale's chances. "Your roommate?"

"It's a wonderful project. In fact, it's similar to your brother's idea, now that I think about it."

"So it's definite? How about Dale? I mean, since I came to the workshop and you know me and all."

She jerked her gaze to him. "You're asking me if I'll play favorites? No. I choose the grants that meet our criteria. The board must approve all grants. If Dale's project is worthy, we'll fund it."

"Sure. I'm only trying to understand how this works."

She blew out a breath. "I don't mean to snap at you.

You're asking the kinds of questions the board might ask. I want to be prepared for that." She looked abruptly troubled.

"You're worried."

"Mostly about our business plan. The one I inherited is a jumbled mess. I don't have any expertise there, so I have to hire a consultant to help me."

At least she didn't expect to get her business model from a crystal ball. That was reassuring. "You know, I could refer you to one of my clients maybe." Or he could do it. He'd worked over plenty of business plans for clients. He could advise her.

And spend more time with her.

"I would really appreciate that. I have to present the plan at the board meeting in a little over three weeks."

"I'll get you a name or two. Sure."

"Thank you so much." She ran her tongue across her lips and made things painful behind his belt. Surely he could squeeze in some time to help her….

One minute she drove him crazy, then the next she got him so hot he wanted to strip her and go at it on the nearest flat surface.

Down boy, he told himself. A mournful howl sounded from down the hall—the dogs giving voice to Mitch's complaint.

"I should let the dogs out," she said.

"I'll move the furniture back." But first he watched her head down the hall, her ass swaying deliciously. The ragged edges of her skirt flicked at her calves like tongues. She was barefoot and he had watched her star-decorated toes grip the floor all night. Did she ever wear shoes?

He could definitely find some time. He needed a challenge.

He'd gotten the sofa in place when the dogs clattered to him, stopping short to snuffle his knees, their small bodies wagging like full-body tails.

"I love these guys." Esmeralda crouched beside him and cuddled each in turn, so close he could smell her perfume and couldn't possibly be expected to ignore the dark space between the curve of her breasts. "I'll miss them when they go."

"Maybe you should adopt them."

"Adopt them? Me? I've never had a pet. I—I don't…" she faltered. "I've always got so much going on. And I expect to do some traveling. And now I have this job."

"Lots of people who travel and have jobs have pets. They board them or hire a pet-sitter." He shrugged.

"I haven't really thought of myself that way." She looked at each dog, then at him, then dropped onto the sofa, pondering the idea.

He was finished. Time to leave. He started to say so, when she looked invitingly up at him. "It's a special night. How about we go out back and soak our feet?"

"Soak our feet?"

"You'll see." She grinned at him.

"It's late. I should go."

"Please."

"Okay." What else could he say when she strafed him with those molten blue eyes?

She filled a pair of art-glass flutes with champagne and arranged a plate with the last slices of star fruit, moving gracefully, almost floating off the floor, jingly softly, hypnotizing him.

He followed her onto her patio, the dogs at his heels, collars clanking, where he saw two white, plastic lawn chairs flanking a small table at the edge of a kiddie pool filled with water.

"This is how I cool off in the summer." She set the champagne glasses on the table, then dropped into a chair with the abandon of a child, gathering her skirt into her lap and plopping her feet in the water. The white stars on her toenails seemed to glow from beneath the shivering surface, reflecting the moon overhead.

The dogs dropped to their bellies beside her chair. "Roll up your pant legs and get in here," she urged.

Mitch put the plate beside the glasses, sat to roll up his pants, then planted his feet in the water near hers.

"Almost as good as having a real pool, huh?" she asked.

"Takes the edge off the heat, all right." He held out the plate to her and she took a piece of fruit.

He gulped champagne to avoid watching her lick the juice from her lips. It was hard enough to hear the wet sound she made.

"At night I lie on my back and let the water tickle my ears," she said, leaning back in her chair, looking very appealing in the moonlight.

"Oh, yeah?"

She looked straight at him, mischief in her eyes. "I do it naked." She put a finger to her lips. "Don't tell my neighbors."

Lust surged through him. "Naked, huh?"

"Does that shock you?" She shifted her body toward him, lips parted, tempting him.

"It does other things to me."

"Oh. That." She shivered. "I know what you mean."

Get out of here. Go home. This will only get harder.

He already was. But this felt so familiar, so right. He felt a rare contentment. He would stay a little longer. To break the tension, he looked up at the sky.

"Remind you of anything?" she asked softly.

"What do you mean?" He turned his head and met her gaze.

"Seventeen years ago we sat on a grassy hill and watched falling stars and ate star fruit." She held up a slice. "Tonight is the first night of the Pleiades meteor shower. Just like then. I read it in the paper. It should start any second."

"Very cool." That explained how familiar this all seemed. The air was thick from the August monsoons, the smell of creosote filled the air and he could hear the crickets rasp.

She took a bite of fruit, the juice glimmering on her lips. Would she taste the same as that night? There was a drip right...*there.* He could just lick it off. It would be a favor....

"Odd that we met again at the same time, don't you think?"

"You mean like it was destiny?" He laughed. "Right."

But she didn't laugh. Her hair fell in silver waves against her collarbone. Both her straps had dropped again and her pale shoulders gleamed in the moonlight.

Her gaze jerked upward. "Oh! Look! There!" She pointed and he managed to catch the fading wisp of a falling star.

The sight of her face, bright with excitement, lips parted sweetly, did something to him. Made his heart heavy and big enough to fill his rib cage. He felt like the kid he'd been, full of wild urges he had to act on or he'd explode.

He had to kiss her.

He leaned over the table, his chair creaking under the strain, cupped the back of her head and pressed his lips to hers.

They were soft as they'd been all those years ago and just as giving. Like a match rasping across the phosphorus strip, he felt an explosive heat, sharp, bright and hot. Hell, he felt like a star shooting across the sky above them.

All he wanted was more.

5

IT WAS HAPPENING AGAIN. Stars were falling and Mitch was kissing her. She was on fire with the rush of it, like a dream come to life. She wanted everything at once— his lips on her mouth, no, her breasts. His hands on her back, no, her breasts. Everywhere. She wanted him around her and inside her all at once. And now.

She wanted their clothes off. And she wanted to tell him what was happening. *We're meant to be together.*

Except there was this tiny inner voice that said, *It's too fast. He's not the same. You don't even* like *him.*

Forget that.

She leaned in, determined to get closer, despite the table between them. He leaned farther, too. Their chairs wobbled. They leaned more. The strain proved to be too much for the plastic legs, which buckled, sending them both into the pool. Mitch's glasses flew off his face and plonked into the water.

She shrieked and Mitch gave a low laugh. The water felt good, sloshing around them. He pushed her hair from her face, looking down at her.

She caught a flash in the sky. Another star flying by. "Look!" She pointed.

He rolled over and together they watched star after

star shoot across the sky. It was like a fireworks show exclusively for them.

"So what does that mean?" he asked. "A bunch of angels get their wings?"

"Or they get laid," she joked.

"I'd rather we do that," he said, looking down at where her silk top clung to her breasts. She imagined her nipples showed.

"Oh, yeah." She sighed, arousal building in her again. "Without your glasses, you look more like Doctor X."

"I'm not him anymore. Not even close."

"You taste like him. Like star fruit."

"You, too." He kissed her, holding her with one arm beneath her back, his tongue searching, lips moving as if he couldn't get enough of her.

She knew how he felt. She pushed her pelvis against him and he slid his other hand down, under her sopping skirt and brushed her between her legs, over the strip of her panties.

She moaned into his mouth, loving that he'd gone there, touched her there, not waiting. She didn't want to wait for anything. Which was so not like her.

She liked to take things slow, set up the room, ease into things. Now she felt desperate. She needed him. It was a drumbeat in her head, a throb along her nerves. She wanted Mitch. Inside her. Now.

Water splashed over the sides of the pool, against their rocking bodies.

You could dry off, go inside, light candles, talk about it.

No. She wanted him out of his pants and inside her.

Right where they were. Now was the time, under the stars streaking the sky.

The dogs whined and circled the pool, upset by the strange human behavior.

What about protection? They had to figure that out. "I'm wearing a patch," she managed to get out.

"A patch?" Mitch looked as dazed as if she'd just declared herself to be a pirate. "Huh?"

"Birth control. I have condoms, too…in my room…." She panted between words.

"I'm healthy," he said. "You?"

She nodded. "So we're good."

"We're great." He pushed up her blouse to cup her breasts.

"Yes, we are," she breathed, arching into his touch.

Is he the man from my past?

She couldn't wait for a psychic assurance that that was true because Mitch had his mouth on one breast and his fingers inside her underwear and she thought she might explode any second. She could only be here, now, feeling all of this.

"In me. I need you in me," she gasped out.

He let go of her breast and shifted to free himself.

She parted her thighs, lifted her hips, practically begging him with her body to enter her.

He eased in, watching her face every second, being sure she wanted this the way he was doing it.

"Yes," she said, craving it. "You feel so good."

"Yeah." He sounded as relieved as she was that their bodies were finally joined. His eyes sparked at her like lightning over a dark lake. Doctor X all over again.

Sort of, she knew. Temporarily.

But enough for now.

He thrust in, filling her. She lifted her hips, wanting more, wanting him deep inside her. This was heaven.

Too soon. Too fast. Not you. The thoughts rose, but she pushed them away in favor of the rush of physical pleasure, more intense than she'd ever felt.

It didn't matter that they barely knew each other, that they were heavy with sodden clothes, that they were emptying the pool with their wild movements, that the porch beneath the thin plastic of the pool was bumpy and hard. Water sloshed, the dogs whined and circled, the stars flew and nothing mattered but this blending of bodies, uniting of desires, this striving together for release.

He quickened his pace and she tightened around his cock, her own body closing in on ecstasy. She wanted to hurry, hurry, hurry and, at the same time, she wanted this never to end.

He thrust in, hard and deep, then out, and her body wanted him back. Again and again. She watched fire flicker in his eyes, aware, also, that he tracked her response, timing his movements to match what he sensed of her condition.

Wordlessly, they read each other, like animals, natural mates, joined by instinct, united in the most vital act of creation.

And then she climaxed, crying out.

Mitch groaned and she felt him let go inside her. She held his wet shirt, locked her knees against his jeans-clad thighs.

He kissed her neck, her cheek, her mouth, as if he didn't want this to end either. "Are you okay?" He pulled her tank top down to cover her breasts, brushed her wet hair from her cheek.

"I'm great. You?" She stopped him from soothing her and slid her fingers into his hair.

"Stunned, I guess." He looked that way. "I'm not sure how that happened."

"It was the shooting stars," she said, fighting the strange feeling that she'd been too far out of control.

"A whole host of angels got their wings and we got laid, huh?" His half smile glowed in the moonlight.

"It was like the first time, only better."

"In a play pool in our clothes?" Huffington licked his face, as if to agree.

"But it felt inevitable, didn't it?"

"Yeah," he said, looking mystified by that, and not exactly at ease with the idea.

Not to worry. I had three readings that predicted this. He'd think she was nuts. Something in her held back, watchful and waiting, and she wasn't going to push it.

Just now, Mitch looked so much like Doctor X. Open and warm and so present. Had she caused him harm that night? "That night, when I did your reading? Did I get it wrong? What happened when you went to L.A.?" she asked.

Mitch laughed, but his body tightened. "The record deal was bogus. The agent was a con artist. He took our money—supposedly for advance work—and blew town."

"And I told you to go, that you'd succeed." She felt sick at the realization. "I was so sure."

"It's a common music industry scam. Lots of people lost a hell of a lot more than we did. Meanwhile, I got accepted to law school and that was where my head needed to be anyway. It was a good lesson."

"But you wanted it so much."

"Every kid with a guitar thinks he's the next rock star," he said. He kissed her forehead, cupped her face. "Forget about it."

"I can't, Mitch. Because the next day I found out I'd got my mother's reading wrong. And it was…awful." Until that day she'd felt invincible. Everything seemed clear and possible and good. She hadn't realized that life could take a horrible turn, that things could go terribly wrong.

"That's why you remembered the date we met?"

She nodded. The next day, her world had cracked and broken apart.

"Want to talk about it?" Mitch asked gently. "Will it help?"

ESMERALDA NODDED. "I think so," she said.

Mitch lay on his side as close to her as he could get, and put a hand on her arm, wanting to comfort her as best he could.

Later, he would kick himself senseless for having sex with her fully clothed in a kiddie pool. It had something to do with being dragged back all those years and feeling a rush of need he hadn't felt in a long time, maybe ever. But that was for later.

For now, he brushed the water from her cheek and vowed to get her smile back.

"I was just learning to read palms," she said, "and I was pretty cocky about how good I was. I read everyone's hand I could grab, including my mother's."

"Was your mother like you? Did she read palms?"

"No. She had some psychic abilities, but didn't develop them. She was a social worker and a counselor, and she said that was a big enough responsibility in the world."

He had a feeling he'd like her mother.

"My gift came from my grandmother. My dad…I don't know about him. He left before I was born, but my mother said if he had any gifts, he'd hidden them from her." She paused and gave a rueful smile. "She wasn't that happy with him."

"I can imagine." He had no respect for deadbeat dads.

"I'd always felt extra energy around people, saw colors, got out-of-the-blue advice to give people. My grandmother helped me understand I was special, not strange. She taught me when to speak up and when to hold back."

"Good for her." Kept her out of a children's psych ward, at least.

"She taught me how to grow my abilities and she showed me palmistry. She only read for family and friends. Her specialty was tarot and chakra healings. When she thought I was ready, she introduced me to Lenore."

"I remember the booth." It was seeing Esmeralda, so pretty and eager, sitting under that painted sign—Lady Lenore, Your Future In The Palm Of Your Hand—that had made him stop there.

"That was my first night with real clients. I did great and then I met you and I was on top of the world." She paused, her eyes shiny. "The next day, everything changed."

He waited for her to continue, the only sounds the

rhythmic plink of the water, the panting of the dogs, the rasp of crickets.

"In the morning my mother sat me down and told me she had ovarian cancer."

"Oh. God." He sucked in a breath. "That's bad."

"I was shocked. I argued with her, can you believe it?" She shook her head at herself. "I'd seen no health problems or an early death in her palm, so it couldn't be true. I was such a fool."

"Don't beat yourself up about it." What a terrible way to learn reading palms was just a game. He couldn't believe she'd ever looked at another hand.

"Lenore explained to me that I *had* seen the truth, but blocked it to protect myself. She'd done the same thing when she met her husband. She'd seen his early death, but shut it from her awareness. When he died of a heart attack at thirty-eight, she remembered what she'd seen."

It sounded to him like self-delusion, but he wasn't about to say that at a moment like this.

"See, when you love someone, you tend to fill in the blanks with your own hopes for the person. You see only what you want to see."

"That's true for all of us," he said, glad of something he could agree with her about.

"Lenore had warned me, but I was too arrogant to let it sink in. My poor mom was so kind about it." She stopped talking and swallowed hard, then managed a smile.

"She loved you." He could imagine the dying woman trying to comfort her heartbroken daughter. He remembered how eager and happy Esmeralda had been the night they met. And the next day…all hell had broken loose. Emotions churned in him, threatening to break through his well-managed cool. He linked his fingers with hers and squeezed.

"After that it was a quick and terrible blur. In two months my mother was gone. I didn't care about anything for a while after that." Silver tears slid silently down her cheeks.

Should he get her out of this stupid pool and dry her off? The pain in her face made him feel angry and helpless. He settled for wiping the tears from her cheeks with the dry edge of his hand. "I'm sorry you went through that."

She smiled. "It's okay, Mitch. Truly. I'm fine now. Anyway, after that, I figured I was a fool to be a palmist. My mother had told me not to stop, but I was so angry and ashamed. I thought I'd lost whatever gift I had. I was numb."

"You had a right to be bitter. Eighteen is young to lose your mom."

"I still loved hands, though." She carried on, unwilling to dwell on her raw deal. He admired her for staying positive. He doubted he'd be as resilient. "So I went to beauty school to become a nail technician. I enjoyed the work, but the whole time I felt hollow, like something was missing from my life."

"You'd lost your mother."

"That was part of it. And my mother helped me figure it out." She looked at him, her heart in her eyes. "Do you believe the dead can visit the living?"

"Not really. No."

"Then this will be hard for you to accept, but a year after she died, my mother visited me."

"You had a dream maybe?"

"Dreams feel different. This was my mother, and she had a message for me. *Don't hide from your gift.* That's what she told me. *Be all that you are. The world needs all of you.*"

He wasn't about to comment on self-hypnosis or trauma-inspired hallucinations. If the "vision" gave her comfort, he was happy for her. "So you started again?"

"A few days later, a nail client asked me to read her palm."

"Out of the blue? That's weird."

"Not out of the blue. That's not the mystical part. She noticed my palmistry book on the shelf behind me."

"Okay." One sensible thing.

"When I read her palm, her lines were as clear as a map. The words came to me like a song I already knew. And, best of all, I felt my mother behind me, her hand on my shoulder, encouraging me."

"Sounds like a powerful moment." He was touched by the emotion in her voice. She believed every word she was saying. She was so different from him. She believed in visions and visits from the dead and telling fortunes and reading auras…and he never would. He believed in what they'd just felt in each other's arms. That was unsettling enough.

"So that was the beginning," she continued. "I got better. Intensified my palm study, expanded into tarot and other readings. And I've never looked back."

"Very interesting."

"You're being polite. You weren't so skeptical when we met. You listened to every word I said."

"You were persuasive. And so pretty. Hell, I would have walked on hot coals if you'd asked me to."

"So you let me read your palm because you wanted to get in my pants?" She was teasing, and he was glad she felt lighthearted enough to do that.

"Do you blame me?"

"Not really. You were pretty hot, too." She sighed. "So that's my story. And now I have the foundation, which means a lot to me. I have to do well. I know this is what my mother would want me to do, to contribute in this way. It's bigger than anything I've ever done."

Her eyes were soft with hope and worry. She seemed so open to the world, as though a stiff breeze could blow her over and she would have no defense against it. He wanted to help her. He *had* to help her.

"Let me take a look at your business plan, Esmeralda. I've seen plenty of them. I know what works."

"You would? Do you have time?"

"I'll make time."

"I hope you have a non-profit rate."

"I'm reasonable. Pull together your paperwork and I'll come by tomorrow at noon and we can go over it all."

"That'll be great."

"Shall we get out?" He got up and helped her to her feet, holding onto her hand for a while. What a simple comfort it was to hold hands. He hadn't done that in a long time. They stood together in the moonlight for a few seconds, dripping water, as if reluctant to end the moment.

Once inside, she went away, then returned wrapped in a thick yellow towel and handed him a similar one.

The mood had changed and they were shy around each other now. He toweled himself down, fighting the idea that all he had to do was flick the twist at the top of her towel and she'd be naked in the golden light of her living room.

"Do you want to stay?" She stood with one bare foot on top of the other, looking as confused by what had happened as he felt.

"It's pretty late," he said. He felt tongue-tied about what they'd done, what it meant. What the hell should he say?

"So, I'll see you tomorrow at noon?"

"Sounds good."

He left her house, carrying his shoes, his wet clothes as heavy on his body as his thoughts were on his brain.

He'd just had sex with the woman who held his brother's future in her hands. Would she make it a big deal? Would she let it go?

Did he want her to?

It had been strange how it happened. He'd heard a roar in his ears and felt such a rush of need he wouldn't have been able to keep from making love to her if he'd tried. Each moan and touch had spurred him on. Her body was life to him, her mouth his breath, and being inside her…heaven.

Unlocking the car, he glanced toward the house and saw that both dogs watched him from the window, ears high, bodies wiggling, as if they expected his return. He kind of wanted to.

He shifted his gaze to the sky and caught a shooting star flying west to east. Someone else was getting laid?

He smiled to himself. What had happened was like some bizarre fortune cookie: *When the stars fly, you will have sex with a fortune-teller from your past.*

In a kiddie pool.

He would love to share the joke with Esmeralda, but she'd probably take it seriously.

He'd promised to help her with her business plan.

Would he sleep with her again? It seemed as crazy as his made-up fortune.

He looked up at the sky and wouldn't have been surprised if the stars had spelled out *Go for it.*

6

ESMERALDA ENTERED Dream A Little Dream the next morning completely confused about Mitch and what they'd done together. All morning long she'd flip-flopped. One minute she felt like helium balloons were lifting her off the ground, the next like she had bowling balls attached to her ankles.

She couldn't wait to see him again, and she wished he'd disappear forever. How could he be the man for her?

He was such a skeptic. She knew the hazards of that kind of relationship. Her friend Zena kept falling in love with non-believers and it was dreadful every time. She ended up second-guessing herself, feeling flat, lost, weak, as though she had to hide her true light from the man she loved.

Esmeralda did not want that in her life. She had enough doubts as it was, without Mitch rolling his eyes every minute.

Though something about him stayed with her. She'd seen that he had a hole in his heart. It had to do with giving up on Doctor X and his music. Maybe that was her mission—to help him get back his hope, his music. Or whatever he needed instead.

She'd see how their meeting went today. Balloons

or bowling balls, she couldn't guess where she'd end up.

When she walked into the office, Belinda beamed at her. "How'd the workshop go?" So chirpy. And Esmeralda was so not in the mood.

"Well, I think. There are a few grants I need you to follow up on." She pulled out the pad where she'd taken notes.

"Hey…wait a minute," Belinda said, staring at her. "You're very…bright. Hold it, please." She waved her fingers in Esmeralda's direction to stop her, then closed her eyes and took a slow, deep breath. She was going to attempt an aura reading.

Uh-oh.

Belinda opened her eyes, then narrowed them, scrutinizing Esmeralda. "Wow. Clear red…lots and lots… and pink…flying everywhere." She gestured wildly.

Clear red meant passion, sexuality and energy, among other things. Pink meant affection, new romance and sensuality. What a time for Belinda to be dead-on.

"What happened last night?" Belinda demanded.

Esmeralda smiled stiffly. "You must be reading the creativity and the stimulation of all the good ideas. Plus, my foster pets. They're dear to me." She fibbed, but she wasn't about to discuss Mitch with Belinda. She had hardly admitted what had happened to herself.

But if Mitch was her man…why not celebrate?

Because of the shoe-waiting-to-drop feeling she couldn't get past, that made her think this matter was far from settled.

"Maybe, but it's more dramatic than that." Belinda tapped her chin, looking suspicious. "Plus, your usual clear blue is muddy. That's fear of the future."

Bull's-eye. Brenda had more of a gift than she'd thought. "It's all the unknown with the foundation, I'm sure. The board meeting. All the proposals. I'd better get at it before the first client gets here."

She slipped away from her assistant's suddenly accurate insights. Her aura seemed to be shouting out what was going on with her like a psychic billboard.

She hoped Belinda wouldn't try to read Mitch's aura when he arrived. Though Mitch was so guarded, she'd never get through the gray. Esmeralda wasn't sure what it would take to get Mitch to put his guard down or if it was her job to try to get him to.

MITCH WAS ALL BUSINESS when he got out of his car in front of Esmeralda's building. There would be no meeting, he'd decided. He'd grab her materials and work solo on the plan when he could.

A sleepless night had convinced him that more sex would complicate an already complex situation. He had yet to hear from Craig about the foundation's legitimacy, though working on the business plan should give him some insider knowledge. Plus Mitch was too fresh from the Julie snafu. This could be one of those rebound things and that wouldn't be fair to Esmeralda.

She was not the kind of woman who took sex lightly and that had to be his mode for a while, he figured, after Julie.

Esmeralda was sweet and somewhat deluded. He would help her with her business plan, push her to fund

Dale's grant and stay clear of those amazing eyes, those drooping straps and that mouth.

Last night's hook-up had been a function of chemistry, the champagne and some bizarre time warp to the past.

And that mouth. Don't forget that mouth.

As sensible as he intended to be, though, he noticed his pulse kicked up at the thought of seeing her again. He could still picture her standing uncertainly in her kitchen, wrapped in that big yellow towel, feet crossed like a child.

He was grinning when he entered the office.

Her assistant looked up. "May I help you?"

"I have a lunch meeting with Esmeralda."

"You do?" The girl checked her computer. She was a younger, shorter, not-as-pretty version of Esmeralda, with bleached hair in stiff ringlets. She wore a gypsy skirt, a top with skinny straps, and way too many bracelets. Where Esmeralda might wear a couple of beaded rings around her arms, this woman had a thick wad around both wrists and her upper arm. It was as if she'd dressed up as Esmeralda for Halloween. Weird.

"Hmm. I don't see a lunch appointment." She suddenly brightened. "Wait? Are you by chance... Jonathan?" She sounded so excited, he almost wished he were.

"No. Mitch Margolin."

"Oh. I see." She drooped in her chair. Who the hell was this Jonathan guy? Santa Claus? A movie star? Someone from the Arizona Lottery with a big, fat check?

"We made the date at the workshop, so she might not have told you."

"I'll let her know you're here." She released a disappointed sigh, called into Esmeralda's office, then sent him there.

Esmeralda left her desk to meet him. "Mitch. How are you?" She leaned in for a hug. He fought the urge to bury his nose in her hair and kept the contact brief and above the waist.

"Fine. Just fine. I can't stay."

"I thought we were meeting over lunch." She looked puzzled.

"Change of plans. I'll take your materials and work on them when I have time. I'll call with questions. When I'm finished, we'll meet to go over it. Sound okay?"

She seemed startled. "Is something wrong?"

"No. I just thought this would be…simpler."

"Simpler?" She hesitated, then her face cleared. "Ah, I see. Last night freaked you out."

"Freaked me out?" He frowned. "No. Of course not. I—"

"It's okay. It freaked me out, too. I don't usually drag men into my play pool and attack them."

He had to laugh at that. "I think it was more of a dump than a drag. It was both of us." She was making this easy. "So, you see my point about keeping things simple." *Whew.*

"Not exactly," she said, her electric eyes digging in. "What are you saying?"

"I don't want us to get into something…you know…" He paused.

She folded her arms, forcing him to fill in the blanks.

"Something neither of us wants."

"And what would that be?" She pinned him to the wall with her eyes. She would make a decent attorney. He could see her in a deposition. *Mr. Margolin, please be specific in your testimony. Precisely what is it you mean?*

"You know." He didn't care to incriminate himself further.

"Maybe I do… Let me see…more of what we had last night? Great sex, you mean? We wouldn't want that, I guess." She leveled her gaze at him, teasing, but not letting him escape either.

"Things are already complex, Esmeralda. I'll be working with you on your plan. And there's the grant to consider."

"And you didn't like losing control. The heat scares you, so you want out of the kitchen. Perfectly understandable." She gave him a knowing smile. "I'll go get the stuff." She spun on her heels, heading for the door, letting her hips sway so that his hands itched to grab them and sink into that soft pleasure.

Slowly he replayed her words. Hey…wait a minute… He'd just been insulted. "Are you saying I'm uptight?" he called to her. "Because I am not uptight. I can be wild." What was he saying?

"Oh, I'm sure you can," she said, then disappeared down the hall, her orange-and-strawberry scent lingering in his head, making him dizzy, making him want to throw her on the sofa and prove exactly how wild he could be.

But that was pointless. She'd given him what he wanted. No sex. Just business. Let it go.

Still, he felt as though he'd somehow lost something.

She returned with a stack of paper. "Let me put all this in a folder." She bent to open a drawer of her desk.

He looked away so as not to see down the deep vee of her purple tank top—straps, this time, but her breasts looked so touchable. He remembered those sweet berry tips…

He busied himself staring at a painting behind her desk. *The Seven Chakras* showed an outline of a human body with glowing blobs of different colors along its midline.

"Here you go," she said, handing him a purple folder.

"Thanks." He met her gaze, her smell filled his head, and he wished they'd at least gotten naked. The sex had been so frantic, they'd missed all the details. And he could use one more taste of that mouth….

"Mitch?"

He realized he'd stood there too long. "Chakras, huh?" He nodded at the painting, as if that was what interested him. "What's that about?"

"Well, *chakra* means 'wheel' in Hindu. These are the radiating waves of energy the body exudes." She ran a nail along the picture.

"All bodies?"

"Yes. Yours, too. Here is your crown chakra." She gestured around his head. "This concerns the brain, of course, and deals with spirituality and self-knowledge. Next is the brow chakra, or the third eye, which concerns intuition and self-responsibility." She made a circle near his forehead, then moved to his neck. "The throat chakra…self-expression and communication." She wiggled a finger at his chest. "The heart chakra, concerned with love for others and self."

She spoke clinically, but the way her hands moved, swirling in the air in front of him, made him feel woozy and overheated, like he was being wrapped in a warm web, tugged closer, pulled in for some soft, pleasurable purpose.

"This is your solar plexus chakra," she said, indicating his belly. "Organs include the stomach and the liver. The issues are self-worth and confidence."

She held his gaze, then dipped her hand to make a circle near his zipper. "Here is the sacral chakra, which, of course, focuses on the genitals and concerns—"

"Oh, I know what it concerns," he murmured. That particular chakra had gone hard as rebar.

She took a shaky breath. "Actually, it's about self-respect and the give and take of energy with another."

But all the same, heat arced between them like a cut power line, flailing around, sparking everywhere. He wanted to hold her, throw her onto her yoga mat and get their chakras moving in synch.

She was shaking, so he knew she felt similarly. Then she backed away. "You're right, Mitch," she said, breathless, as if the moment had gotten away from her. "I don't understand what's happening with us, but I don't think it's a good idea to push it. Call me when you've looked over the stuff." She gestured at the folder.

"Sounds good."

"How did it go with Dale? Is he working on the grant?"

"I blew it, I guess. I got on his case about missing the workshop, and he got defensive. He'll never even read the notes I took now."

"Would you like me to talk to him? Would that help?"

If anyone could snag his attention, it would be Esmeralda. "He'd probably listen to you. It would be great to get you two together." And Mitch would have to be there for introductions.

He was an idiot. He should be grateful to escape her magnetic field of loonyness, but he couldn't wait to see her again. "He's playing at a supper club tonight. Come for dinner with me. That way we can make the meeting casual."

"You're asking me to dinner?" She looked puzzled.

He was, too, but he wasn't backing out now. "And if I get through this—" he held up the folder "—we can discuss it, too."

"Sure. And I'll bring my tarot cards, maybe read Dale's palm?" She was teasing him.

"Whatever it takes to get him a grant."

"You might come prepared to dance under the moon. Naked."

"Like I said. Whatever it takes."

What the hell was he doing?

ESMERALDA STOOD AT BELINDA'S desk watching Mitch walk away. They had a date. She couldn't quite figure out how it happened. He'd marched in, declared their relationship strictly business, and then, when she agreed with him, asked her on a date. To talk to Dale, of course, but still.

She was nervous. The energy between them was very powerful. She'd been merely explaining chakras when the swirling heat, the rush of lust, had taken over. She hadn't even gotten to the foundational chakra. She'd have to explain that to him tonight.

Tonight, when she'd see him and—

"Esmeralda?"

She dragged her eyes back to Belinda. "Huh?"

"I asked if you'd like me to bring you a falafel?" Belinda followed her gaze, still aimed at Mitch's retreating form, then stared at her. "For lunch? Hello?"

"No. Thanks, anyway. I brought a salad from home."

"That was a quick meeting."

"What?" She dragged her eyes down to Belinda.

"Is he a client? Mitch Whatever." She nearly sneered his name. Why the attitude?

"No. I mean kind of. His brother is applying for a grant, which is why he came in. But he's a business attorney and he's agreed to work on our business plan for us."

"He just offered and you accepted?" Her voice rose.

"He's experienced."

"But did you get references? What does he know about our mission, anyway?" Belinda's outrage made Esmie remember that Belinda had offered to help with the business plan. She'd even brought in a book— *Starting Your Own Business*—which rested now beneath the palmistry and tarot books on her desk.

Esmie had just ignored her offer and gotten a consultant. Clearly, Belinda was hurt.

"I'm sorry, Belinda. I know you offered to help with that, but you and I would be starting from scratch. Mitch already knows what we'd take weeks to grasp. I have to save time where I can to be ready for the board meeting."

"I guess that's true."

"I have an idea, though. I want you to go ahead and screen the proposals for me. You can test the rubric and then give me your recommendations. It should save me time. How about that?"

"That'd be nice," she mumbled, assuaged a bit.

Esmeralda should depend on her more. Maybe her twinges of intuition were wrong and Belinda was more capable than she thought.

"So when will this Mitch guy have the plan ready? Should I set up another meeting?"

"He might have something for me when we get together tonight." *Oops.* Too late, she realized how that sounded.

"You're going out with him? Do you think that's wise?"

"I think it's just fine." *And none of your business.*

"But don't you want to keep your eyes out for…you know… I mean, if you get involved with someone else, what happens when *he* gets here?"

And maybe he's already here. "I'll worry about that when the time comes, Belinda," she said, not sure at all what she should do. Maybe Belinda was right. Maybe Jonathan might still arrive. Maybe that was the fluttery feeling in her chest.

Or maybe it was the fact that she'd see Mitch again.

MITCH COULD NOT TAKE HIS EYES off Esmeralda at the supper club that night. She stood out against the tropical background of the place in a white dress with no straps at all, only a flimsy lace shawl that hid nothing. So much worse than those spaghetti thingies.

She'd swept up her hair, but some strands bounced against her neck when she laughed and moved. And she laughed and moved a lot. She was so…wiggly.

The makeup or lotion she wore on her shoulders and chest held glittery flecks like fairy dust. She looked edible.

The bamboo table was small, so they sat close, bumping knees, their faces inches apart.

He'd been so transfixed, he'd let her coax him into a girlie cocktail—a prickly pear margarita, which she said had "resonance" in her life. As soon as it arrived, he ditched the plastic stirrer and the twist of sugared lime and a prickly pear jelly. He had to hold on to some shred of masculinity.

The woman had purely bewitched him.

He wanted steak, but she started an argument about beef abuse, so before the waitress got bored, he settled for the salmon she insisted had omega-3 and antioxidants that would extend his life. How could someone who looked like an angel be such a pain in the ass?

She enjoyed everything, though. Exclaiming over the decor, the menu, the margarita, telling him how much she loved jazz. "This is so fun." She wiggled into her chair, making her shawl fall off her shoulders.

He caught his breath. "Watch it." He gestured at her neckline.

"I thought falling straps bothered you." She tilted her head at him, then wiggled her shoulders. "It won't slide down. See?" She had to know how the sight affected him, the soft rocking of her breasts under the fabric, her bare shoulders inviting his touch. Every time she took a breath, he saw a tantalizing extra millimeter of skin.

"Wouldn't want you to catch a chill."

"Oh, I feel great." She pulled back her shoulders and he watched her nipples tighten into sweet knots.

He crossed his legs. That damned sacral chakra was taking charge. Now she was licking the sugared rim of her glass. *Good Lord.* He looked toward the door, relieved to see his brother heading in with his stand-up bass. "Dale!" He waved him over, desperate for the distraction.

His brother nodded at him, then put his instrument on the stage and returned to their table. "Hey, bro," he said. "I didn't know you were coming tonight."

"Esmeralda McElroy, meet my brother Dale," Mitch said.

Dale's gaze shot from Esmeralda to him and his grin

broadened. He nodded knowingly. *Finally scored, huh?* If curiosity kept Dale around long enough to get infected with Esmeralda's can-do attitude, Mitch wouldn't care if the guy thought they were engaged.

"Have a seat." He motioned at the chair.

"What's this?" Dale said lifting the purplish drink.

"Prickly pear margarita," Esmeralda announced. "My favorite. Want one?"

"I'll pass," he said. "I can't believe you've got my brother ordering an umbrella drink." He gave Esmeralda a high-five. "I wish I had a camera." He picked up the jelly Mitch had discarded and bit it. "Tangy." He looked at Mitch: *You dawg*.

"Yeah," Mitch said, "Anyway, so I was talking to Esmeralda about that grant idea—"

"I'm so excited to hear you play," Esmeralda interrupted.

Mitch felt a sharp pain in his instep and realized Esmeralda had stabbed him with her heel. To shut him up. He leaned down to rub the spot.

"Mitch says you play a lot of gigs, that you're getting your name out there."

"He said that?" Dale's gaze shot to him.

"Of course I did. You're good." He rubbed his foot.

"And that you do some studio work?"

"I've played on some albums, yeah. Done some advertising." He shrugged.

"Really? Where would I have heard you?"

Dale coolly rattled off an impressive list of credits, shrugging when Esmeralda made a big deal about how in demand he was and then about how many downloads his band had from MySpace.

Mitch got impatient. Dale's set would start soon and Esmeralda hadn't said a word about the grant.

Still, it was clear that Dale was warming up to her, his face softening with pleasure as they talked. Soon she had him talking about how much he liked the kids he gave private lessons to, especially the geeks who blossomed with their musical abilities, began dressing better, acting cooler, actually getting dates.

Mitch was impressed with his grace and assurance. Dale sounded like an adult, not Mitch's little brother.

Esmeralda listened with her eyes steady on Dale's face, taking him in, holding him, reading his heart, it seemed. She had a way with people, that was clear. Maybe that's what being psychic was all about—an excessive sensitivity to people. That didn't mean she was a nut case, right?

Before long, the drummer signaled Dale and he headed for the stage. Hell, he hadn't even hit Mitch up for a beer, which he always did when Mitch came to hear him play.

"That was more than he's told me about himself in two years," he said to Esmeralda when she turned back to him.

"I just listened."

"Which I evidently don't. That why you stomped my foot? To shut me up?"

"You said you tend to push his buttons."

"Very true." He sighed. "So at the break, you'll talk about the grant?"

"I have a better idea." She looked toward the door and smiled. "And here she comes now."

He turned to follow her gaze and saw that Annika, Esmeralda's roommate, was headed their way. He hadn't talked to her during the workshop, but it was impossible not to notice her dressed all in black, with piercings everywhere, her black hair streaked orange and a laugh that filled the room.

Esmeralda waved her over. "I thought since their grants were similar it might be smart to put the two of them together."

"You're good," he said, thinking that Annika was definitely Dale's type. "All this and a matchmaker, too."

"I do my best."

Their eyes met and he felt a charge that made him glad Annika was heading their way. Eventually, however, they would be alone and he'd have to get control of his impulses by then.

Annika arrived. She wore a T-shirt that said Eat The Rich, big rhinestone earrings and purple lipstick. She and Esmeralda chattered away about the foster dogs and a neighbor named Jimbo who had hit on Annika and a parrot Annika wanted to buy that knew twenty-four songs on cue. The two women leaned toward each other, laughing so hard they choked on their drinks.

Annika was all drama, but it was Esmeralda who had him riveted. If that energy chakra thing were real, hers were shooting off light and heat and color like one of those paint spinners at the state fair.

When the band started to play, she moved to the music, managing to dance with only her upper body, which wreaked havoc with his shaky control. "There's something about jazz, you know?" she said. "The energy is slippery…it gets into your system, makes you hum."

"It's good." But it wasn't the music making his system hum.

In a bit, Annika headed for the ladies room.

"Isn't she a doll?" Esmeralda said. "Funny and smart and intense."

"She's all that, but we want Dale to work with her, not sleep with her, right?"

"Maybe your brother needs to mix work and play."

"That seems to be his mode."

"Maybe you could learn from him."

"What do you mean? I have fun. I enjoy my life."

"Do you?" She leaned in, digging at him. "Do you enjoy your work as an attorney? What exactly do you do?"

"Sure I like it. I help companies with incorporations, buy-sell agreements, real property leases, equipment leases, employee rights issues, sometimes lawsuits. The usual legal stuff."

"But you work with new companies, right? So you fulfill dreams, too."

"Hardly. I file a lot of papers, give advice."

"But it must be creative. I mean you'd have to have a creative outlet, being a musician and a writer and all."

"It's mostly problem solving."

"But that's creative." She seemed to be trying to convince herself he hadn't fallen off the right path.

"I'm fine, Esmeralda. I'm happy."

"At least you're having fun now," she said softly.

"I am."

"Maybe that's why I'm in your life again."

"Does there have to be a reason?"

She smiled a mysterious smile, as if she was right and he was clueless. He was almost ready to believe her.

Almost.

When the set ended, Esmeralda introduced Dale to

Annika and Mitch watched the chemistry experiment fizz like Alka-Seltzer, spilling out of the beaker and all over the table.

Annika asked about Dale's band. Dale asked about Annika's degree in art therapy. Annika mentioned her grant, and Dale immediately suggested they combine projects. After all, music was definitely therapy and he'd always been into art and a joint project would be more impressive. Annika suggested getting together to pin down a budget and Dale rattled off a bunch of cost factors that proved he'd thought this through far more than he'd let Mitch know.

It all clicked into place, as if they'd scripted it. Mitch's jaw just hung there. Esmeralda looked like a cat who'd scored all the cream in the dairy.

He wanted to kiss her out of gratitude.

Hell, he plain wanted to kiss her. As the night wore on, she'd become more and more irresistible. Every flick of her hair or glance got to him. Watching her fingers twiddle the cocktail stirrer, he could have bench-pressed the table with his cock.

When his brother went up for the next set, he leaned close to her. "Looks like I won't be needing that naked dance under the moon, after all."

"And I was so looking forward to that."

"Yeah," he said, picturing her naked with him, turning slowly, arms outstretched, the moon making shadows and shimmering shapes on her sweet body....

"I believe our work here is done," she said. "I think Annika and Dale can take it from here."

"Home then?" he said, the word resonating in him, as if home was a place they shared. He shook his head.

Maybe the tequila had gone to his head, though he'd been drinking water for the past two hours.

All the way to Esmeralda's house, Mitch breathed her in. She'd put the shawl on her lap and the passing lights and shadows of trees and buildings flew across her bare shoulders, making her seem otherworldly, making him want to touch her to be sure she was real, a warm woman beside him in his car.

This, he knew, was insane.

He parked in her driveway. She immediately opened her door, as if to end the evening. Disappointment stabbed him, but she was right. They'd agreed that sex would complicate things.

Perversely, he insisted on walking her to her door. He helped her out of the car, holding her hand again just for the pleasure of it.

At her porch, she turned to him. "I had a lovely time." She had to extract her hand from his grip.

He'd held on too long. Where the hell was his social sense? "Thanks for talking to Dale. You handled him exactly right. You're good with people. No clairvoyance required."

"Who says that's not how I did it?"

Looking at her face, that wisp of a smile, those lips, he had no interest in the debate. "Could be," he said, just to keep her smiling at him.

"You're coming around, Mitch," she said. "I'd say that calls for a shooting star." She looked up at the sky.

He looked, too, amazed to see a meteor skim by on cue, the trail so broad and big it looked staged. More followed, one after another, a dozen stars streaking the sky like a laser show for them alone.

"I'd say that was a sign," Esmeralda said. "Wouldn't you?"

"Yeah," he said. Anything could be a sign if you wanted it badly enough. And he wanted her. Badly. Something came over him, a force beyond his own will—fate, desire, a momentum built of the hours together, he didn't know or care. He only knew he was going to kiss her and he didn't want to stop soon.

When he touched her lips with his own, she made a soft sound and leaned in, welcoming his mouth, and he held her in his arms, her angel dress as soft and thin as a second skin. They kissed for what seemed like hours, hanging onto each other for dear life. They needed to get inside. Find a flat surface. Ditch the clothes.

Reading his mind, Esmeralda broke off long enough to fumble her key out of her satchel and unlock the door.

Inside, they ignored the dogs to keep kissing in the golden light of her living room. This was wrong, but it was what he wanted now.

Later would just have to take care of itself.

7

IT WAS A SIGN, Esmeralda thought, melting into Mitch. Not the meteors, of course. That was predictable astronomy. The sign was Mitch's admission that she *might* be clairvoyant. He'd stopped bristling and arguing about her skills. He trusted her, and that was a sign that this was right.

At least she hoped it was a sign, because she was too aroused to stop. She was submerged in sensations. Mitch tasted of the tangy drinks they'd had, and he smelled of his spicy cologne and outdoors and of him, his skin, just him.

Wild desire gathered in her, like an animal crouching to spring into the air.

"Where's the bed?" he managed to say between kisses.

She waved an arm behind her toward the hall, barely able to stay on her feet. There was a continent of furniture between here and there, so when she backed into the Early American monstrosity she simply fell onto its stiff cushions.

"Good idea," Mitch said and took her mouth again.

His glasses bumped her cheek, and she pulled them off and dropped them to the carpet so she could see his eyes at full power. White-hot desire gleamed from the dark brown of his irises, taking her breath away.

Mitch went for her mouth, tugging her into the swirl of heat and need, and she was soon trembling and moaning, desperate for more, but somehow unable to do anything but hold on and keep kissing.

Mitch was more sensible, going to work on her zipper, getting it far enough down that he could uncover her breasts. "You're so beautiful," he breathed, then sucked a nipple deeply.

She gasped and arched upward for more, liquid below the waist, loving the wet give of his tongue and lips on her breast, pulling at her, taking her down and down.

She felt as though she was starving for him, that she would die if she couldn't have him, just fade away in despair. She rubbed against him through his pants and her dress, wrapping her legs around his thighs. There were too many clothes. She wanted to run her fingers across his chest, feel the muscles of his back, tangle her legs with his, touch him.

"Get this off," she cried, tugging at the hem of his shirt. He whipped it over his head and tossed it to the floor. She had a second to take in the tan muscles, round nipples, streak of brown hair leading to his belt, which she went after.

Except he went for her zipper again, getting her dress off, leaving her in her yellow bikini underwear.

He gripped her hips, surveyed her panties like they were the last barrier to the world's gold. "Nice," he said, then yanked them off so fast the fabric scraped her flesh.

She was naked now and he took in the length of her, and she was glad they weren't covered in water-logged clothing in her play pool. Her bed would be better. The couch arm kinked her neck and there was something lumpy beneath her, but then Mitch shifted so he was kissing down her belly and his hot breath sent chills down her legs and she…couldn't…quite…care….

He ran his tongue around her belly button.

"Oh…what are you doing?"

"Putting my mouth on you. Sound okay?"

"Sounds great." She reached down to grip his head. He traced the top of her pubic curls with his tongue, sending licking flames along her nerves so that her legs went rubbery and seemed to disconnect from her body altogether.

"But what about you?" she moaned, wishing he could feel this same glory.

"We'll get there. This is for me, too." He dipped his tongue to lick her spot.

"Oh. Oh. *Oh-oh-oh.*" She nearly leaped off the sofa, banging her head on the arm. If there was pain, she couldn't feel it.

He swirled his tongue around the tip of her clit, making it ache at the sudden pleasure. She felt so very *naked.* To his touch, to the brushing heat of his tongue. His fingers dug into her upper thighs, then stroked her, adding to the sensations from his lips and tongue. She rocked her hips against his mouth.

He made a noise of contented pleasure, which aroused her so much that she was ready to come.

She wanted to warn him, say something, but she could only moan and fight for breath.

"Yeah," he breathed against her sex, obviously sensing where she was. With a final sweet tug of his lips he sent her over the edge. She made wild sounds and thrashed beneath him. Somehow he managed to stay with her.

This was so good. So *good-good-good*.

How could she be so lucky? To have a body, to have this man pleasure her with such willing skill, to feel every bit of it, to feel so good? When the last wave had subsided, she spoke through a huge exhale. "Oh, thank you."

Mitch chuckled at her extravagant gratitude. He kissed each of her thighs in turn, then kissed up her body. She welcomed his mouth, enjoying the intimate taste he'd retained of her.

She'd just had an incredible orgasm, so she was surprised when Mitch's kiss was like match on fresh tinder. Lust whooshed through her, hotter than hot all over again. As if they'd barely touched.

This time she wanted him naked and inside her. She reached for his zipper, but he shifted away and took care of his pants himself. He rose over her and she parted her legs, eager to receive him, lifting her hips, welcoming him inside her. She loved the warmth of his body, his power, the way he loomed over her, so strong, so male. He moved with easy strength in and out.

She ran her palms across his back, loving the way they rocked together, bodies meeting, separating, then meeting again for more. She loved the full feeling, the glory of their union, the amazing luck of this experience.

Just as she'd thought, sex with Mitch was more intense than she'd ever experienced. She wanted to slow down and she wanted to speed up, she couldn't get enough, would never get enough.

"Esmeralda," he said. His face changed when they made love. Gone was his cool detachment, replaced by fire, by close attention, subtle sensitivity to her every move and glance. He was utterly tuned to her and to how they were together. This felt right, this felt perfect.

He was her man, her future. They strove together, bodies moving as one, connected, joined in body and spirit.

Mitch stilled, captured her gaze, held her there, on the brink of release. She wanted to move, to go, but he held her there, made her wait. *Feel this, wait for it, let it build.* She ached to leap off, to shatter, to fly. When she thought she couldn't stand a second more, he took a quick, short stroke deep into her. She shot off like a released spring.

She cried out. So did Mitch and he held her tightly, the way he'd kept his mouth on her when she climaxed, as they rode the wave of release, gliding, swimming, tumbling through the thick, liquid moment.

When it was over, she felt as though she'd thudded to earth on this hard and boxy sofa, which had kinked her neck, by the way. And what was this lumpy thing? She pulled one of Pistol's chew toys from under her hip. It squeaked sharply. Mitch's knee landed on her thigh. "Ouch," she said.

"Sorry." He scrambled to relieve the pressure.

She shifted her body, trying for a comfortable angle on this terrible sofa to cuddle with Mitch. He tried to help, but they were suddenly all elbows and knees and bruised shins.

Her phone rang then.

"It's pretty late for a call," he said.

"It might be an emergency," she said, struggling to her feet because she never screened. Someone in need might give up in despair, lose the courage to ask for help. This was probably someone she'd pinkie-sworn to call her if they'd had too much to drink and needed a ride home from a bar.

She picked up the phone. "Hello?"

"Thank God you're still up." It was Annika. "I need you to pick me up. I'm at the police station. Dale, too."

"You're what? At the police station? Dale, too?"

Mitch had joined her and he put an arm around her, listening in.

"What happened?" she asked.

"It's a mess," Annika said. "We were frickin' profiled. I was driving Dale home and some nimrod slammed on his brakes. I just barely whacked him, but this cop stops and thinks I'm some Goth meth head and, of course, here's Dale with long hair, which makes him a dealer. Christ. So they searched the car—no warrant, no probable cause—and Dale argued and I wouldn't do that humiliating nose-touch sobriety thing, so they brought us in."

"Are you being charged with anything?"

"No. They were just being macho assholes. I got a ticket just for being behind an idiot. It wasn't my fault and—"

"So it's just a ticket then. I'll come and get you." She got the station address and hung up.

She put her arms around Mitch. "So, this is good night, I guess?" She squeezed him, wishing they could keep going, never have to stop and think or figure anything out.

"I guess so. I'll tell Dale you gave me a call and that's why I'm picking him up."

Why keep their being together a secret? Except she

felt the same way, and what did that mean? But Mitch kissed her and she wanted to forget everything else. His arms around her, he pushed her back against the table, she shifted her body and—

Beep! "You have thirteen new messages." The mechanical voice of her phone machine was like a splash of cold water. She'd bumped Play with her hip.

"Thirteen messages since we left?" Mitch said.

"Someone could be in trouble."

"I'll get dressed," he said on a sigh.

The first message was Belinda, and it came just after they'd left for dinner. *Call me as soon as you return.* Something about the mount of Mars she didn't understand. A palm-reading emergency? *Please.*

The next message was a friend asking for advice. As Esmie listened, she watched Mitch pull on his pants, the sexy sight of his bare upper body in tight jeans making her shiver. *Mmm.*

Jimbo needed her car to take his mom to the doctor… a friend wanted a daisy cutting…someone else wanted a reading.

Mitch nimbly closed the buttons on his sexy shirt.

Her friend Autumn's voice drew her attention. "Esmie, got the date of my farewell performance at Moons. Sugar's coming from San Diego. We'll dish. Can't wait to tell you how right you were."

Autumn and Sugar were her best friends. They shared a birthday, which they celebrated each year. Autumn had recently quit her popular burlesque revue in Phoenix to be with the man she loved in tiny Copper Corners. Even though Esmeralda had predicted major changes in Autumn's life, the dramatic outcome was startling.

His clothes on, Mitch approached, holding out her dress so she could step into it. She did, listening as Jewel said she still wasn't sure about living with her boyfriend, which meant the ugly furniture would stay a while longer.

Mitch zipped her up with slow care and she leaned against his chest, listening to the rest of her messages—two more requests for palm readings, an invitation to a baby shower, then Jill. "I've got someone interested in Huffington, Esmie. Call me back and we'll set an appointment for a pickup."

"Oh," she couldn't help saying, stabbed by disappointment.

"Someone's taking Huffington?" Mitch asked.

"Adopting him. That's what happens when you foster pets."

"So decline. Keep the dog." He bent down to rub the top of Huffington's head, then Pistol, who was waiting for his turn.

That was impossible. She'd signed an agreement. This was how being a foster owner worked. She didn't respond to his suggestion, just listened to the machine, which had recorded three hang-ups, a half hour apart.

"Somebody wanted you bad," Mitch said.

"They were on the half hour, that tells me it's Belinda. Persistent and orderly."

"What did she want? Something about a mountain?"

She laughed. "The mount of Mars. That's part of the palm. I'm teaching her palmistry."

"That's generous of you."

"I'm happy to do it." But she felt tense, what with Mitch leaving without really talking about this and all the people who needed her flooding into her awareness.

"You don't look that happy. You look stressed." He put his arms around her. She wished they were naked again, submerged in mindless pleasure.

"I'm just a little overwhelmed, I guess."

He held her quietly and she soaked in the comfort. "You've got a lot of maps on your walls," he mused. "Maybe you should take a trip."

She had itineraries and travel books to go with the maps. That had been a hobby of hers and Jonathan's; planning trips, studying the countries, cooking the foods.

"I will. When the time's right." When she felt prompted to go, when her friends and clients didn't need her so much.

"You're waiting for a psychic message?" It was a gentle tease, but it hit her wrong.

"What's wrong with that?" She turned to meet his gaze.

"When you want something, go for it. Take charge."

"Timing is important. You can push something and ruin it."

"You can wait forever. Time flies."

"Think about Dale. When you pushed him, he balked."

"Not the same thing. And you're being inconsistent. Look at your workshops. You tell those people to seize their dreams, not wait. Why can't you do the same thing?"

"That's not relevant. That's—"

"We're doing it again," he said softly.

"Doing what?" she asked, then realized what he meant. "Arguing. Yes, we are."

"This wasn't supposed to happen tonight," he said.

"I know." She'd turned his lust-inspired concession into a sign. She was doing what Zena did, falling for a skeptic who would argue her into a negative swirl of self-doubt. The true sign was their argument and their mutual confusion.

"We'd better pick up the jailbirds, I guess," he said, "before they actually get arrested." He stroked her cheek. She couldn't read his emotions. Regret? Doubt? Hope? She had no idea. But that was only fair, since she couldn't read her own feelings either.

"YOU NEVER CALLED ME BACK," Belinda said the minute Esmeralda stepped into the office the next morning, her head aching from lack of sleep.

"I got in too late." She was not in the mood to be grilled by her bubbly assistant.

"You did? You worked late on the business plan?" She asked as though it was her last hope.

"We didn't get to that, no."

"Oh. I see." Her face sank. "Mitch left a message on the machine, by the way," she said glumly. "You're to meet him for lunch at Café ZuZu. Noon. He wants to go over the business plan and *things*." She said *things* like it was something scandalous.

The fact he'd chosen a public place meant he wanted to be sensible. That was good…right? Esmie couldn't tell if she was relieved or disappointed. Her uncertainty was unnerving.

She felt as if she was holding her breath, paralyzed, frozen. The restaurant he'd chosen, in the newly renovated Valley Ho Hotel, was only a block away, an easy walk. She'd just see what happened when they met.

She had finished early with her eleven o'clock meeting when Olivia called. "*Cara,* how is the best foundation director in the universe?"

"Just fine, Olivia." Her extravagant compliments made Esmie a little uneasy. "How are you?"

"Hungry. Let me take you to lunch today and you can tell me everything. I want you to see a new line I noticed on my palm."

"Today? I, uh, have a meeting today. With a consultant. It's about the business plan."

"Oh. Well. That's important, I know. I had such a craving for spinach tortellini. So we'll talk when I come in for my nails on Saturday. In the meantime, you're thinking of fifty grants to present at the board meeting?"

"Fifty? Um, we'll try."

"We need to show those tough old *birbantes*—those rascals—what we can do. What a cranky bunch. Sometimes I wish my brother was not so pushy with his cronies."

"I'll do my best."

"You'll have everything spelled out, the *T*'s dotted, the *I*'s spotted, right, *cara?* I know you will. You're so good. I dreamed how good you would be."

Each gush from her benefactor raised Esmeralda's blood pressure. Olivia's message was *make me proud* and Esmeralda wanted to do that more than anything.

"As I said, I'll do my best."

"Of course you will. And you'll have the business plan set right and some fund-raising ideas, too, I know. Because you are always ahead of me."

"Absolutely," she said, her throat closing up. She hadn't gotten to fund-raising ideas, though she hoped Mitch would have some suggestions in the plan he was working on.

She wanted to be worthy of Olivia's confidence. But *fifty grants?* She'd approved only ten so far. She was glad now she'd asked Belinda to prescreen. She'd have her shorten the appointment times to a half-hour, then give herself twenty minutes to read grants between sessions. She counted on the appointments as her chance to tune into the client, verify the grant's potential, sense the success. Shortening the time would make it difficult, but it had to be done.

She had to be successful. For Olivia, for her clients, for her mother and for herself. And what was that about? The foundation made her feel…legitimate. Which she knew was wrong. Being a palm reader was a worthy calling. But she had her own negativity to deal with. That was why Mitch's criticism had made her anger flare, enflamed her deepest doubts. Maybe he took her back to when she'd failed her mother.

She also had bristled at his remarks about her not traveling. He'd made her thirteen messages seem like an indictment, not an honor, though he had seen her weariness.

That gave her an uneasy tightness in her heart chakra, something she was blocking from her awareness.

She had no time for a personal crisis. There was too much on the line. Mitch was only making things worse.

Belinda popped in, carrying a stack of folders. "You've got twenty minutes before your lunch meeting, so would you see if I'm in synch with you on these grants?"

They'd only begun when her cell phone rang. It was Jill, and they set the pickup date for next Wednesday— just six days away. Jill was enthusiastic about Lindy Little, the woman who wanted Huffington. "I think I talked her into taking Pistol off your hands, too."

"Pistol? Oh, he's no trouble. I love him."

"But the two dogs are close, right? It would make a better transition for them both. They'd have each other."

"True. You're right." Her heart plummeted to the floor. Hanging up, she felt faint.

"Are you okay?" Belinda asked.

"I'm fine." Or she would be as soon as she could take a breath and the room would stop closing in on her. Huffington *and* Pistol gone? No more greetings at the door, their whole bodies wagging? How could she bear it? Belinda was talking, but Esmie was struggling to calm down.

She could never do this again. She was not brave enough to foster another pet.

"So, the teddy bear grant seems good to you, too?"

"Good? Uh…" Belinda had been going over the grant, but Esmie hadn't heard a word. She fought for focus, pushed away her thoughts about the dogs and about Olivia and the board meeting and Mitch. She blocked out the sadness and worry and alarm.

You do that a lot, a voice inside her said. But she had to set aside her own issues to help people. That was part of life. *You don't look that happy. You look stressed.* Mitch mixed her up, made her wonder about herself.

"I'm sure it's fine," she said to Belinda, blowing out a breath. "I've got to scoot. If you think a proposal should be funded, put it in my yes stack and make the appointment. We need to shorten the appointments, too." She explained the situation, happy that Belinda would take over from here.

She would just have faith that her assistant could handle all she'd given her, ignore the spikes of doubt.

She had no time for doubts, not if she was going to succeed with the foundation.

Even running all the way, she was ten minutes late to ZuZu's. She dashed into the dim lobby of the Valley Ho, breathing hard. There was Mitch checking his watch, looking every bit the impatient attorney who saw dollar signs with every passing minute. How irritating…

Except he looked devastating in an expensive suit, crisp white shirt with cuffs. Her racing heart did a header into her stomach. She still wanted him.

When he caught sight of her, she saw he wanted her, too. His face softened, his mouth moved, and heat gathered in his eyes, clearly visible, despite the barrier of his glasses.

He dragged his gaze away and frowned at his watch. So that was how he would be. All business, no emotion. Probably just as well.

"Sorry I'm late," she said. "I got held up."

"We need every minute," he said grimly, raising the leather portfolio he held. She could see her purple folder sticking out.

Her heart sank. The plan must be a worse mess than she'd feared.

The hostess took them to a booth in a private corner, but Mitch objected. "We'll need more light. Maybe by the window?" He gave the hostess an I-know-best smile. He wanted a well-lit table to avoid any hint of romance, she was sure.

"So how are you?" she asked, determined to be friendly.

"The business plan is a mess," he said, sounding almost angry. Like a physician blaming the patient for an illness.

"Which is why I needed a consultant," she said, trying to stay cool.

"Not to put too fine a point on it, but are you sure your predecessor wasn't out-and-out fired?"

"Why would you say that?"

He flipped open the leather binder, then her folder and whipped through the stapled pages. "This is completely blue sky. Inflated figures. No demographics that make any sense." He turned the printout toward her. "Here. Can you see…?" He twisted his head, couldn't read it upside down, frowned, then came around to sit beside her on her bench.

She was instantly aware of his scent, the brush of his thigh, his strength beside her.

He cleared his throat, as if the contact had startled him, too, and shifted slightly away from her body. "Look at the budget. Extremely unbalanced." He tapped at the columns of expenses, promotion, interest income and other items, then turned a page. "The research isn't annotated. There are no market strategies, no competitive analysis. And the financials are eight months old. I'll need recent numbers to get anywhere."

He gave her an accusing look.

"Belinda is working on the accounts. Come back to the office with me after this and I'll have her print you a report."

"I have to say the whole plan looks like someone fired up a bowl and dreamed it up."

"I know you're doing us a favor. And I told you this wasn't my area. If this is too much work or not what you expected, say so and we'll find someone else."

"This is just worse than I expected," he said, soften-

ing his tone. "I'm sorry I came on so strong." He gave
her a speculative look. "How did she get the job? Your
predecessor?"

"You mean, did she read palms, too?" She couldn't
help being sarcastic. She'd expected help, not the third
degree. "I have no idea. I didn't ask."

"You didn't ask?" He paused. "Where did Olivia
Rasbergen get her money, by the way?"

"I don't know. It's family money, I think." Olivia had
mentioned her sister-in-law Bianca's yarn business as
an example of little ideas that had turned out well.
"What does that have to do with anything?"

"I would think you'd investigate a company before
you took a job. Find out who runs it, check their back-
grounds, make sure everything's on the up and up, that
the place won't fold in six months." His tone was both
angry and patronizing.

"I trust Olivia, Mitch. Why are you so suspicious of
everyone? And why are you talking to me like I'm an
idiot?"

"I'm not. I'm trying to look out for your interests. I
don't want to see you in trouble or disappointed. I know
you mean well, but—"

"But I'm a flake, right? I'm psychic, I don't have
a business degree, so I'm clueless. Look, if you're
going to hammer on me and Olivia and the foundation,
then let's just forget this. I'll pay you for your time and
we'll be done."

He looked stricken. "I'm sorry. I keep saying things
wrong." He put his hand over hers, which sent a sweet vibration all down her body, melting her anger instantly. It
was ridiculous how changeable her reactions to him were.

"What's going on here?" she said.

"I don't have the faintest idea." His business edge disappeared, and he looked completely lost, which made her feel less alone.

They looked at each other, breathing hard, electricity crackling between them, heat rising in a flood, until it seemed like their booth could float away with them in it.

"Last night was…" she said.

"I know. It was."

A beat of intense desire passed between them.

"Ah, Esmie." He grabbed her arms and kissed her.

She kissed him back, madly, wildly, right there at the sunlit table by the window, oblivious to the other diners, the wait staff, the passersby.

Mitch broke away. "What are we doing?"

"What we're supposed to do." What else could explain it?

He kissed her hard, his arms tightly around her, as if holding on would save both their lives.

She was glad. If she didn't keep touching him, she might cease to exist altogether. She kept trying to surface, come up from this drugged desire. *What are you doing? This is not you.*

Where had this wildly passionate person come from? None of her sunny lovers had brought out this crazy possessiveness, this desire to lose herself in another person.

Mitch seemed to forcibly pull back from her mouth. "We're getting a room." His dark eyes simmered with banked heat, and all she could do was nod. The Valley Ho was a hotel. *Perfect.*

Mitch threw bills on the table for the meal that hadn't yet arrived and led her to the lobby reception desk.

8

IT TOOK A *MONTH* TO CHECK IN, Esmeralda thought. This was so extravagant, spending a hundred and fifty dollars for a mere hour in a hotel room. Summer rates, at least. Maybe they'd just give up their respective afternoons and spend the night.

This was so crazy. So not like her. Not like Mitch, either, she was certain. Which had to be the sign she'd been waiting for. Feeling this strongly about someone meant it was right.

While the clerk ran his credit card, Mitch held her close, running his hands up and down her hips so sensually she almost moaned. She wanted to wrap herself around him and rub against him like a cat in heat.

This was why people got crazy about sex. This feeling. This rush, this flood of hunger, the desperate sense that you had to connect, be naked together or you might just die…or certainly pass out from the strain.

It was scary, but it also filled her with wonder. She looked up at Mitch while he initialed all the *X*'s for checkout time and credit card charges. Everything about him turned her on. The strong line of his jaw, the way his crisp collar touched his hairline, the perfect knot of his silk tie. She felt woozy with desire.

This reminded her of her first hormone-driven middle-school crush on a rock star. She'd craved his music, his videos, stared for hours at his poster, had desperate, embarrassing fantasies about meeting him, touching him, kissing him, so that her vision went gray and she'd nearly sobbed with the agony of so much desire coursing through her bloodstream. Every cell, every fiber of her being cried out for the man—his look, his voice, his words, his being.

It had been hormones, of course. The big flood that had blown all her circuits. Eventually she'd stabilized, settled in to a normal libido and a friendly interest in sex.

But here it was again, that first overwhelming, bubbling soup of desire. She practically quivered with impatience as the clerk asked whether they wanted one key or two. "One," she croaked out, sounding so desperate that both Mitch and the clerk looked at her as if they feared she'd need a paramedic.

Mitch pressed her against him with one arm. "Almost there," he whispered in her ear, his breath sending waves of goose bumps down her body, all the way to her fingertips and toes.

Somewhere music played too loudly, a tinkling song. *Turn it off,* she thought. It got louder and louder until she realized it was her cell phone ringing in her bag.

She decided to ignore it.

Mitch accepted the key folder and gathered her against him.

"Thank God," she said as they rushed out of the lobby to where the rooms formed a two-story quadrangle around a grassy area.

Her heart raced. In a few seconds they'd be behind a

locked door making love. What about her two o'clock client? Somehow it would work out. She couldn't care. They just had to *get in that room.* It hadn't even embarrassed her when Mitch declined the offer of a bellhop for their nonexistent luggage.

"One-seventy-seven. This is it," Mitch said, shoving the key card in the door, then opening it.

"Sevens are lucky for me," she said.

"Me, too," he said. "Now." He swung her into his arms.

She giggled like a girl, delighted to be swept off her feet, as if he were her groom, or a vanquishing lord.

Her cell phone rang again.

"Let it go," he said, backing into the room with her in his arms, taking her mouth with his.

They stood like that, kissing, Mitch holding her against his chest, for long minutes, letting the pleasure build.

Her cell phone went off *again.*

She ignored it, but Mitch broke off. "Maybe it's an emergency."

"It can wait." She didn't dare admit an interruption. This moment might not come again. "I'm taking charge."

"Good girl." Mitch lowered her feet to the floor, then took her satchel from her arm and dropped it, too.

Wordlessly, they stripped each other, the only sound their harsh breathing, the slide of fabric, the rattle of his buckle, the scrape of his zipper. The air was cool, the light deliciously dim.

Soon Mitch stood naked before her, broad and handsome and strong. She felt wonderfully safe. Which was odd. Her psychic gifts and the white light that surrounded her warded off any danger. But it felt good to know that Mitch would never let harm come to her. She could depend on him, he would be there for her. It was a feeling she hadn't known she wanted.

"What's on your mind, Esmie?" He kissed her softly, his fingers warm on her upper arms. He'd started calling her Esmie.

"I feel good with you," she said, her throat tightening with emotion. "Different."

"Me, too," he said, taking her hand in that possessive way he had. "I can't get enough of you." He led her to the bed and they lay down together, on their sides, bodies as close as they could get, breathing each other's breath, hearts beating in time.

The sheets were cool and crisp beneath them, the air brushed their bodies, the curtained dimness softened the edges of everything so the moment felt like a dream.

Mitch pulled her even closer, his arousal pressing against her, reminding her of the pleasure to come. They kissed, taking their time, not frantic now.

She shifted her body so he could enter her while they lay on their sides. Once he was deep within her, she released a breath of relief, as though she'd been waiting forever for this.

Mitch used slow, deep strokes, while she rocked with him, wanting to stay as close as possible. She breathed in his smell, felt the power of his muscles, loved how their bodies strove together, tensing, releasing, eager to reach the peak, prepared to jump as high and wide as they could manage.

"I look at you and I want to be inside you," Mitch said into her ear. "I don't understand what's happening."

I do, she almost said. *It's our destiny.* But something

in her still held back, that shoe still hovered overhead. She closed her eyes, fought off the doubt, focused on the building rush of her climax, marveled at how their bodies moved like two halves of a whole. The wonder of it put tears in her eyes.

Mitch stilled, as if he'd sensed her impending release. He read her so well. He looked into her eyes, and she saw how much he held back, how much heart he had, and that he'd made himself vulnerable to her, even though it scared him.

She was so touched. "Mitch," she whispered tenderly.

"Esmie." He pushed in deeply, as if he knew where her switch was and that she wanted it pressed. Her orgasm took off.

Mitch surged, too, so they sailed together through the wild pleasure, the waves pushing them out and out, then down and down until they landed softly on the big, cool bed.

Her heart hadn't even stopped pounding when her cell phone rang again. She wanted to scream.

Mitch chuckled. He stumbled out of bed and brought her satchel to her. He shook it. "This thing weighs a ton. What have you got in here? A crystal ball?"

She tended to overload her bag. Tarot cards, books, crystals, office supplies, toiletries, this and that. "I like to be prepared," she said, refusing to defend herself. She fished out her phone.

The display said "office." Her next appointment wasn't until two, and that was a half hour away. If Belinda wanted her to explain the Simian line, there would be hell to pay. "Yes?" she said, steadying her voice.

"Thank God!" Belinda sounded breathless, but

with happiness not alarm. "We need you back in the office A-S-A-P."

"We're, uh, meeting." She glanced at Mitch, who grinned, his teeth bright in the soft light of the room.

"This can't wait. You *want* to be here. It's an emergency. A good one."

"Belinda...I can't leave right now...." Why not? She *had* to cuddle? That seemed ridiculous in the middle of an important work day. She looked at Mitch.

He shrugged and bent for his pants.

"I'll be there right away," she said to Belinda and hung up. "She says it's a good emergency."

"We need to get back," he said, leaning in to kiss her.

"I guess so." She realized she didn't want to return to the real world, where what they'd just done might not seem so perfect and right.

He handed her dress to her. "I'll drive you back to save time. I can grab the financials from your secretary."

They both dressed quickly, keeping their separate thoughts to themselves. She was unnerved by her reaction to the call. Psychic impulses were racing along her nerves. The emergency felt as if it had something to do with her and Mitch, but how could that be?

By the time they'd reached the foundation door, Esmeralda was trembling all over, the way she felt when a huge premonition was about to come true.

"What's wrong?" Mitch caught her by the upper arms. "You're shaking like a leaf." He squeezed, as if to steady her, to let her know he was there.

"I'm not sure," she said. She noticed a smear of her lipstick on Mitch's neck and wiped it off, then straightened his collar and his tie.

"We'll figure it out, Esmie. Somehow." He smoothed her hair on both sides, ran his thumb under each eye, as if to remove flecks of mascara.

"I look okay?"

"Good enough to eat." He managed a smile, but she could tell he was feeling jumpy, too.

She smiled back, fighting that skittering sense of dread.

Squaring her shoulders, she took a steadying breath and pushed through the door.

What met her eyes made her heart stop and the floor seem to jerk out from under her like a yanked rug.

Standing beside Belinda's desk, beside a vase of dyed daisies was…

"Jonathan?" She nearly fell back against Mitch.

"Surprise!" Jonathan's eyes lit with delight.

"Why are you…? How did you…?" She couldn't move. A tingle ran down her spine and something shifted into place, like a chiropractor making a skull-rattling adjustment. *Clunk. Pop. Thunk.* Here was what she'd been waiting for.

"It's the man from your past!" Belinda blurted. "Isn't this great? Just like I predicted. He's here."

Jonathan lunged forward and threw his arms around her in a hug she was too stunned to return. He pulled back to look at her. "It's so good to see you."

"It's good to see you." She'd always loved his cheer, his energy, his warmth.

But Mitch was behind her, a wall of silence. What must he be thinking? "I'm sorry," she mumbled, turning to him. "Mitch Margolin, this is Jonathan Walters, my—" she paused "—my ex-husband."

Mitch inhaled sharply, so she rushed ahead with the

introduction. "Mitch is a business consultant...and a friend," she said to Jonathan.

The men nodded at each other and mumbled greetings.

Esmeralda felt embarrassed and guilty, but whether about Mitch or Jonathan, she wasn't sure. Her energy was flying madly, spinning and spitting. She hardly knew what to think, do or say.

"I'll be going," Mitch said abruptly. "If you could get that information to me," he said to her, all business, "I'll keep working on the plan."

"Okay...I'll do that." He was gone so fast she couldn't have said anything more if she'd tried. He was surely upset. Why hadn't she mentioned she'd been married before? Because what had happened between them had been so fast and furious they hadn't said a word about past relationships.

Were they even *in* a relationship?

Meanwhile, Jonathan was here. He'd returned. He beamed at her and held out the vase of flowers. "I remembered that daisies were your favorite."

She nodded numbly, accepting the vase of fading blooms. Jonathan had always been sentimental. But she could still feel Mitch's kiss on her lips, his protective arms around her body, making her feel so...so...

Stop it. Jonathan is here. And just when she'd concluded Mitch was the one. She felt suddenly woozy. "Come into my office," she said.

"Shall I cancel your two o'clock?" Belinda said, eager as a puppy. "So you can spend time together?"

"I don't want to disrupt your life," Jonathan said to her. "We have all the time we need. After work is fine."

Jonathan wanted to take *time?* That wasn't like him.

He looked different, too. Taller, somehow, and his eyes were clearer, his gaze more direct. She liked that.

"We'll talk until the client arrives," she said to Belinda and led Jonathan to her office. She set the vase on her desk and turned to him.

"You're as gorgeous as ever," he said. "Maybe more gorgeous."

"You look great, too." He was still handsome, with that killer smile, deep dimples and high energy. The sight of him alone used to cheer her up.

"But you can tell I've changed, right?"

"You do seem different." More solid and more confident. More powerful than before. His aura when they'd met had had tons of yellow with huge vibrating streamers of abstract tan, making him unusually lighthearted and childlike, with scattered energies. If she could read him now, she'd bet the tan had faded. He seemed to have settled into himself.

"I am. And I intend to prove it to you."

"You don't need to prove anything to me, Jonathan."

"I've missed you, Esmie. I didn't realize how much until now. I wouldn't let myself feel it because of how it ended, because of how I let you down."

"That was a difficult time." Her head spun with thoughts of the past, the divorce, the predictions, Mitch and now Jonathan. Both back again. She fought for air. Her emotions swirled and slid and scooted away, like when she tried to read the aura of someone she loved. Hopeless and confusing.

"I have to sit down."

Jonathan caught her gently by the elbow and led her to a chair, where he sat and grasped her hands, loosely linking fingers. Friendly. *Hey, how about we hang together?*

Mitch held her hand like he'd never let go. Possessive. *You're mine and don't forget it.*

Stop thinking about Mitch.

She looked into Jonathan's face. Sexual interest surfaced in his blue eyes, then wisped away, like clouds before a breeze. He seemed a little puzzled for a second.

"This is a shock," she said, feeling numb. "After six years, to see each other again."

"I know. Except you had a prediction, right?"

"How did you know?"

"Belinda told me all about it. She insisted we call you from your meeting. She said I'd come in the nick of time."

"She said that?" She meant Mitch, no doubt, fearing that Esmeralda was getting involved with the wrong man.

"We had quite a talk while we waited for you. I think it's so cool that she predicted my return."

"Well, she didn't exactly…it was 'a man from my past.' No one by name." Why did it matter? *Stop explaining.*

Jonathan had always believed in what she did, and he'd supported her fully in exploring her gift. Unlike Mitch, who could barely hide his disdain for her life's mission.

Stop thinking about Mitch.

"My newspaper in San Diego picked up the story about your foundation from the wire. I had already wanted to see you again, but I was waiting until I could pay you back."

"You don't have to do that, Jonathan," she said. "Money isn't important." Though it had been agony at the time. Six months into their marriage, Jonathan had lost all their savings on a bogus investment.

"But you lost the house you loved." The money was to have been their down payment, and she'd been heart-broken. Jonathan had big ideas and the financial sense God gave a grasshopper, spending two dollars for every one he had, meaning well every minute.

"I have a lovely home now. And a terrific landlord. I'm more of a renter-type person, anyway. I intend to travel." She remembered Mitch's jab about her putting that off. Maybe she'd been waiting for Jonathan to return.

"You're making excuses for me, Esmie."

"I discouraged you at every turn. I know it was hard to talk to me about your ideas after a while and—"

"Stop." He put a finger to her lips. "I didn't have the courage to own up to my weaknesses, but I'm not like that any more."

She'd been so critical that he'd stopped sharing his wild money-making ideas. If she'd been less dismissive, he might have told her about the investment and she could have talked him out of it. This was her regret—that she'd criticized, not guided.

He reached into his blazer and brought out a check-book. "I had it all planned. I'd write you one fat check for the whole amount—but I'm afraid it will have to be in installments for a while. I'm putting everything into developing my business."

"Don't." She covered the hand that was holding the checkbook. "That was a long time ago. It was your money, too." He'd left a note, then sent the divorce papers a few weeks later. *I want you to move on, to live the life you deserve, free of my mistakes.*

"I'm on the right track now, Esmie. I got a life coach, and he's taught me a lot about honor and commitment.

I know my strengths and weaknesses and I can admit my failures. I was such a bullshit artist."

"You believed in what you did, and you never cheated anyone."

"But I wore rose-colored glasses. Not anymore. I've started a company. Travel Experiences. Remember our travel plans? This sprang from that. I started it three months ago. I'll be taking tourists to countries for volunteer projects in developing countries—tutoring kids, building housing, staffing community centers and preschools. Vacations That Make A Difference is my tagline. I even have a few investors."

"That sounds wonderful, Jonathan."

"It does. But I'm not rushing it or getting grandiose. Bankruptcy is a heavy reality check."

"I'm glad you're being realistic."

"And I will pay you back. That's important to me."

"There's no hurry at all."

He smiled a smile that lit up his eyes and turned his dimples into deep shadows in his cheek. "I should have known you'd respond this way. You are such a good person, Esmie. I've felt so guilty for so long I put off contacting you."

"I never meant for you to feel guilty."

"I can see that the prompt to come now was dead-on. Bad timing or no."

"Bad timing?"

Jonathan shook his head to indicate it was a small matter. "I postponed a trip to Costa Rica to finalize the arrangements for my first tour group. If this is the time I'm supposed to see you, then I'm glad I'm here."

Jonathan had been prompted to come? That was curious and certainly an indicator that their reunion was meant to be.

"I'm glad you're doing well, too, Esmie," Jonathan said. "You have this important job and Belinda says you're swamped with grant requests."

"I'm excited about it, though the business aspects worry me a little, to tell you the truth."

"You'll figure it out. You always do."

His support warmed her, though it was based on pure hope. Tons better than Mitch's questioning her judgment at every turn.

"It's good to see you, Jonathan," she said, tenderness flooding her. They'd been so compatible. The sex had been fine and fun and energetic. Nothing like it felt with Mitch.

Stop thinking about Mitch.

She *was* glad to see Jonathan, to smooth the jagged edges of their breakup, erase the blame. She felt like a balance had been restored.

"That's music to my ears." He paused. "Are you seeing anyone?"

"Kind of." Was she seeing Mitch? More like sleeping with him.

"But it's not serious?"

"No. Not serious." She didn't know what it was. White-hot flame and irritating arguments.

"Good," he said and took her hand again. "I don't know if we could get back to where we were, or even if we want to, but I'd like to try."

"I would like that," she managed to say. "To try, I mean." If they were meant to be together—if Jonathan was the man from her past—it would soon become clear. She'd get past the numbness and feel that rush of love and desire.

What about Mitch?

The minute she said yes to Jonathan, she wanted Mitch. Her libido wasn't quite ready to shift gears.

If only she'd waited with Mitch, instead of jumping in with both feet. She'd done that before—wrestled a prediction into a shape she wanted, trying to control it instead of letting it happen as it would. She brought her eyes to Jonathan's, hoping he couldn't read her doubts.

"We still have feelings for each other, but we're not sure what they are, right?" he said.

"Exactly." Relief flooded her. Jonathan had doubts, too.

"We'll spend time together and see how it goes." He sounded so patient and sensible that she felt much better.

"How long are you in town?"

"As long as it takes," he said in the expansive way of the old Jonathan. Then he ducked his head. "Not exactly." He smiled sheepishly. "I do need to get to Costa Rica soon. But I'll be back. And you can visit me in San Diego. We'll work it out. No pressure." He smiled again, flashing white teeth, deep dimples, his energy lifting her spirits. Jonathan had been so easy to be with. Now they could *begin anew.*

"So, can I take you to dinner tonight?" he asked.

"I'd like that, except I need to talk to…"

"The other guy. I understand completely." He smiled. "Tomorrow night is fine." He wrote down the hotel where he was staying, and she took the slip of paper.

"Aren't you proud of me?" he said. "In the old days,

I'd ask you to break it off now and I would want to sweep you off for a five-star dinner and a bottle of Cristal."

"That's good," she said.

"I know important things take time. It's like Belinda was saying to me, if you rush your life, you miss living it, like watching the scenery from a train."

"Belinda said that?"

"She's very wise. She reminds me of you." Something flickered in his eyes, some puzzlement about that. Probably the way Belinda imitated her hair and the way she dressed.

"And I'm on a budget, too," he added. "No more 'live rich to become rich.' Now it's 'watch the pennies and the dollars take care of themselves.'"

"You've come a long way, Jonathan."

"It means a lot to hear that from you, Esmie." Without warning, he leaned forward and kissed her.

It felt…

Nice. Warm. But there was no wash of desire, no melting heat. Still, Jonathan was familiar. She knew his mouth like the back of her hand. Which was what it felt like to kiss him.

Stop that right now.

"So, I'll wait for your call about tomorrow night," Jonathan said. He was such a warm, tender-hearted man. He understood her without having to say a word.

Not like Mitch, who made her work every minute.

And set her on fire.

Stop thinking about Mitch.

Belinda announced her two o'clock client, so Jonathan left.

Esmie stood for a minute and fluffed the daisies he'd

brought. The poor things had no idea they would shrivel and droop in hours. She closed her eyes.

Jonathan had returned, just as she'd hoped, and she felt…disappointed. She'd go home and light some white sage to clear her energy. A solid meditation and she'd be able to see Jonathan with new eyes.

The timing was good. He'd arrived before she got too deeply into Mitch, who did not fit with her in all the ways Jonathan did. She should feel relieved and happy. But she felt sick.

And now she had to call Mitch and tell him whatever they'd been doing was over.

"THERE'S AN ESMERALDA MCELROY on the line." Maggie's voice startled Mitch through the intercom.

"Take a message, please."

"You have time for a personal call, soldier."

"How do you know it's personal?"

"She told me."

"I see." He hoped to God Esmeralda hadn't given Maggie any details. The last thing he needed was Maggie in on another of his personal miseries. "I'll have to call her back."

"Sheesh." In a moment, Maggie was back. "She'll stop by at five."

"At five? I'm swamped."

"I told her you'd be done by then, and you should be."

"Fine," he snapped, then felt bad for shooting the messenger. "Sorry. Thanks, Maggie."

"She sounded very nice. Warm. Considerate. Smart and—"

"Stop right there. It's not like that." It was much

worse. Just Esmeralda's name felt like a punch in the gut. He couldn't stop thinking of her in the arms of her cow-eyed ex-husband.

The guy had brought her cheap flowers, like a loser on a blind date.

Why would Esmeralda marry the guy? He was too short, for one thing. With surfer looks and a baby face. And dimples, for God's sake.

But Esmeralda had seemed thrilled to see him. *Thrilled.* How come she hadn't told Mitch she'd been married?

And when exactly might she have done that? When he was practically dragging her by the hair to the hotel check-in?

This whole thing had gone way too fast. It stunned him that she'd made him forget his afternoon clients, hell, his own name. He could still smell her orange-strawberry scent, still feel the silk of her lips, the slide of her sex.

Why did women like those stupid cheek dents? The guy had probably had plastic surgery to get them, too. Esmeralda was such a softie she probably didn't see how phony he was.

Oh, Mitch was in a black mood. He shook his head, tried to clear his brain, get his internal organs under control. They were staging some kind of riot. His stomach clenched, his heart banged around, and his lungs were not cooperating at all.

She was coming at five. And, like the fool who would hold an unrequited crush on an associate for months, he was dying to see her, hoping against hope she'd blow off Jon Boy and they'd go back to where they'd left off.

And where was that? Before her ex showed up, he'd

been trying to think of how to explain that he wasn't into anything serious at the moment, that they should go easy, see where it went…. Yeah, right. What a jerk.

Three hours later, Maggie called in to tell him Esmeralda had arrived. He fought the urge to barrel out to her and forced himself to stroll casually to the reception area.

"Come on back," he said to Esmeralda, with a neutral smile, barely glancing at her for fear one look at her sweet face and his cool facade would crack clean off.

"I'll hold all your calls," Maggie said with a wink.

"It's after five. You should go home." No way would he let her stick around to eavesdrop, as she obviously wanted to.

"Okay, I guess." She'd grill him in the morning for sure.

He led Esmeralda to his office.

"Very nice," she said, scanning it quickly, fingering the purple folder she held.

"It does the job." He'd furnished the place in generic elegance. Landscapes on the wall, cherry wood bookshelves, desk and armoire. Pricey wallpaper. Brass lamps. Brown leather sofa and matching wing chair. Fake plants in the corners. No personality really.

"Maggie said you're very busy. And very good."

"Maggie's great. She keeps me on target."

"I brought the financial information you wanted." She held out the folder, her hands shaking a bit.

She was avoiding the real purpose of this visit, which meant he wouldn't like what she had to say. Dread filled him, but he put the folder down without looking at it and caught her gaze. "How are you?" he asked softly.

"A little thrown. I didn't know Jonathan would show like that."

"But you did expect him." He realized with a jolt that was what he'd noticed. She didn't seem that surprised.

She looked startled. "In a way, yes. One day. Not today."

"Yeah, well, these things happen."

"The thing is…that…he wants…rather, we want…"

"You want him back?" His voice was too sharp. He softened his next words. "I can see it in your face."

"I don't know, Mitch." Her voice held a gratifying amount of anguish. "We broke up abruptly over a misunderstanding. We didn't really give ourselves a chance."

"So, now you can."

"And I think we should try. To be fair."

"God knows you have to be fair." He was being an ass, but he couldn't seem to help it. A pressure was building in him and his organs were in that damned uproar.

"You're angry. And I understand. I just can't divide myself, and you and I, we only had—"

"Chemistry. Yeah. I get that. No big deal. Where would it lead, right?"

"That's just it. I don't know where it would lead or exactly what I feel. It's so new…." She was gnawing her sweet lip again, and he wanted to suck the soft pillow into his mouth.

He dropped his gaze, but there were her breasts with their plump tips that knotted against his tongue. He wanted to hold her so close they couldn't tell each other apart. He wanted to consume her, be consumed by her. *What about us?* Something in him cried out to ask her that. They'd hardly started, dammit. What about their chance?

"I'm not sure what will happen with Jonathan," she

said softly. "Maybe it won't work out." She swayed closer, feeling the pull again, too, her powerful eyes shiny with emotion.

His pulse pounded in his ears. He could sweep her up and carry her…where? The leather sofa? Stiff and sharp-angled, but it would do. He had to change her mind.

Then he stopped himself. This was insane. He didn't want leftovers or a mercy hope dangled in front of him. "Be with him," he said. "If he's what you want, go for it."

"But, I don't—"

"I'll draft the plan," he snapped. "Maybe one meeting and a few phone calls and that'll take care of it." He wasn't about to spend any more time with her than he had to now.

He was mouthing sensible, efficient words, but he felt as if life was draining out of his body, leaving him empty and frail.

Just ego, dammit. She'd slammed his ego in a door, and it smarted like hell.

"If you think that's best," she said softly.

"So is he psychic, too, or something?" he blurted, hating himself for wanting to know.

"No, but he supports my gifts. He believes in me."

"There you go. That's what you want." It made sense. Let her ex-husband shuffle her tarot cards and ask her to predict the future. Mitch would never be able to go along with that.

"I've hurt you. I'm sorry."

"What are you talking about? We had great sex. I have no complaints. Would I like more? Sure. Who wouldn't?" He shrugged, as if it was no big deal, hating himself for the lie.

"Don't pretend it didn't matter, Mitch. I didn't intend for this to happen. And if I could change it—"

"Look, we're clear. You're doing the right thing. Now, I'm way behind on this brief, so…"

Her eyes flashed with hurt. "Why do you have to be so hard, Mitch? This isn't easy for me, either."

"I don't see the point in dragging out the inevitable," he said, softening his voice. He didn't want to hurt her. "Fish or cut bait, you know?" He cupped her cheek. "I don't know. Being with you felt…"

"Inevitable? I know. It did to me, too."

He looked into those turquoise flames of hers that seemed to see him to his bones and sighed, his whole heart in it. "Do what you have to do, Esmeralda."

For a woman who thought she could read minds and predict the future, she looked remarkably unsure of herself. He had the decency not to point that out. In fact, it gave him a shred of hope, like the last fiber of a fraying water-ski rope, when you knew any second you'd be hitting the wake face first.

When she finally broke eye contact, he thought he'd be relieved, but he felt like someone had ripped out his heart. A kind of liquid pain ran along his nerves, and he had the awful feeling it wouldn't go away for a while.

9

THE NEXT DAY, ESMERALDA looked up from the batch of proposals she'd gone through. She'd disciplined herself to keep to the new shortened schedule that allowed grant reviews between appointments. It meant sacrificing some of her psychic powers, but she had no choice if she was to meet Olivia's goal of fifty grants for the board meeting in three weeks.

She'd asked Belinda not to disturb her until noon, when Jonathan was due for lunch.

She hoped when she saw him this time, it would all become clear. So far, every time she thought about Jonathan, she remembered Mitch. She kept reliving making love with him in the soft light of the hotel room, side-to-side, face-to-face, the connection sexual and so much more.

Something about Mitch reached her deeply. His solid assurance, his steady bead on the world made her feel centered. They could laugh together. When they set aside their differences, they enjoyed each other.

But their differences. That was the problem. Mitch couldn't even admit he was hurt that she'd ended it. He had to come on all tough business guy. *Let's cut our losses, be realistic.*

Please. She'd seen the vulnerability in his eyes when they'd made love. He cared.

But enough about Mitch. Now she and Jonathan had a chance. At the moment, she felt as muddy about the two men as she had when she'd faced Jonathan, Mitch at her back.

Last night, she'd tried to clear her energy with a sage-smoke smudge and a longer-than-usual meditation.

Of course, it hadn't helped that her phone had rung off the hook all evening and she'd had to say good-bye to Sonny and Cher. The two cats were clearly going to a good home. The vibe had been steady and golden from the lady who'd picked them up. The cats had seemed relieved to be away from the two dogs.

Who would be leaving her in a few days, too.

Esmeralda's heart pinched with pain at the thought. She rubbed her tension-tight neck, did a head roll and a shoulder hug to release her breathing.

It was noon, and where was Jonathan?

She headed out front to see if Belinda had heard from him. From the hallway, she could see that Jonathan was sitting beside Belinda's desk. Their heads were together studying something…his palm, which Belinda held, a palmistry book open under one elbow.

She was reading his palm. How sweet.

"Don't worry, though," Belinda said in a conspiratorial tone. "It was just animal attraction. Which was why you *had* to come now."

Great. Belinda, in her well-meaning nosiness, had told Jonathan about Mitch. She fought irritation.

"Esmie's so lucky to have you," Jonathan said.

"I don't know if she agrees." Belinda blushed and

looked down at his hand. "Let's check out your relationship lines, shall we?" She seemed more relaxed with Jonathan than Esmie had seen her during a reading.

Esmeralda felt a spike of guilt. Had she contributed to Belinda's insecurity? She stayed where she was to give Belinda a chance to finish.

"Let's see... Here's your relationship with Esmie. It fades...and on your fate line there should be a...wait. There's no break for your divorce. That's odd." She looked up at his face.

Jonathan seemed alarmed. "Really?"

"Maybe because you held her in your heart?"

"Probably," he said uneasily. He shifted in his chair.

"Oh. Wait." She frowned again. "There's a new relationship starting soon. It's deep and strong. And there are children." She shot him a glance, then bit her lip. "I must be misreading it. Hang on." She turned to the palmistry book and began to flip pages.

"That's fine, Belinda," Jonathan said. "You gave me plenty of good news. I should go get Esmeralda."

"I hope I helped you," Belinda said, allowing the book to close.

"You did. You saw my growth and my new business. I liked how you put it. 'Feet on the ground instead of head in the clouds.' Very poetic."

"That was good, wasn't it?" She beamed at him.

Jonathan beamed back. There was a beat of something...energy...warmth...something unusual...

Before Esmeralda could get a bead on it, Belinda caught sight of her and leaped to her feet. "Esmeralda. Hi. Jonathan got here early and we were talking. He let me, uh, practice."

"That's great," Esmie said, smiling to reassure Belinda. "Shall we go to lunch?" she said to Jonathan.

Esmeralda led him to her favorite vegetarian restaurant, and they sat at her usual sunny table, where the shadows of outside palm trees flickered on the lace cloth, making it seem alive. She breathed in the familiar aroma of hummus and garlic, cinnamon and cloves. "I hope you like the food here."

"If you like it, I'll love it." He smiled the smile that never failed to warm her.

"You were always so easy to be with." Jonathan never ordered the hostess to a certain table or argued with Esmeralda about omega-3 and the dangers of eating too much beef. "We never argued." She sighed, remembering the bliss of their early days.

"Esmie," he chided. "You forget all the fights about money and all my schemes."

"They were plans, not schemes, and we only fought at the end when I became so controlling."

"Remember when I wanted to be Rocket Man, going to elementary schools with toy rockets as a physics lesson?"

"That was a darling idea."

"Except I forgot about liability insurance."

"You couldn't know everything at once."

"I should have done more research before I bought all the supplies. You warned me, too."

"I'm just glad I found someone to buy the chemicals. I think the neighbors thought we'd built bombs in the backyard."

"I was a schmuck, Esmie. My coach said so many

things that you had said to me and I just blew off. You were the sun in my life, but I hid in the shade."

"It wasn't that bad. Neither of us was perfect. We had a lot of fun. Remember the travel game?"

"Of course. My favorite was Greece. We made feta?"

"And it turned out like snot?"

They both laughed. She loved his laugh and his eyes, so warm and clear, she almost wanted to kiss him. This was a good sign, she thought, and she felt less anxious about their reunion.

"And the wine? The first batch tasted like vinegar, the second like French fries."

"Yes. That was why they told you to use new containers."

"Who knew?"

"I liked the collages best. I still have them up. I kept all the itineraries, too."

"I can't believe I never took you on any of the trips."

"We traveled—San Diego, Flagstaff, Tucson."

"Come on. We planned trips to Greece and Italy and Spain and Ireland. I was so full of pipe dreams. But now I can take you everywhere. I get discounts on tours. I'll make it up to you, I swear. We can travel the world."

"We both made mistakes, Jonathan. I loved making the plans." Had she ever believed they'd go? Would she ever travel? Had Mitch been right? Was she being passive? He didn't know the whole story, but he didn't care. He was Judge Mitch, pounding his gavel, declaring her a fraud.

Forget it. Enjoy the moment. The memories she and Jonathan had just shared made her smile. She was beginning anew with the man from her past. Forget Mitch, who was an opinionated pain in the butt.

"You always made me feel good about myself," Jonathan said, gently taking her hand. She had the annoying wish that he'd grab it, make her know how much he wanted her.

Stop comparing. She was done with Mitch.

"This feels good, doesn't it?" Jonathan said. "Being here together, sharing a meal."

"Yes," she said. He was so much easier than Mitch. Except she felt a sharp pain behind her eyes, which meant there was a truth she didn't want to see.

"What's wrong?" he asked, leaning forward in concern.

"Nothing. Just a small headache."

"Headaches mean something for you, Esmeralda." He studied her. "It's about us, isn't it?"

"It might be. I don't know. It's so sudden."

"Come here." Jonathan leaned across the table and kissed her. It was pleasant, and he tasted of mint and tea. She waited for a surge of heat, but she felt... friendly.

Jonathan ended the kiss, then seemed to be evaluating it. "We're both tense, I think." He smiled. "We're not rushing anything, remember?"

"That's good." Maybe it was the pressure of expectations. A watched pot never boiled, right?

But where are the fireworks? a voice inside whined.

Maybe when you were mature, you didn't need fireworks.

And maybe this was Mitch's fault. Maybe all the sparks and heat had worn her out. Maybe her sexual feelings were sleeping it off, taking a breather.

Maybe Jonathan was right. It would take time.

The ache behind her eyes intensified, so that when

the waitress arrived, she ordered hot peppermint-chamomile tea for its analgesic properties.

"So Belinda did a good job reading your palm?"

"Excellent. She picked up on my growth, too."

"I'm glad to see her be more confident."

"She's a sharp cookie. She's going to hook me up with a morning talk show producer in town to promote Travel Experiences. She had good ideas for my Web site and suggested working with educator groups. Very smart."

"I'm glad to know that. She needs to find her strengths. I think I make her nervous."

"She worships you."

"I wish she wouldn't. I'm no saint. I make mistakes."

"Not very many," he said, giving her the old adoring look. It made her uneasy. She'd forgotten that. Jonathan put her on a pedestal, treating her as though she was wiser and better than she was. She preferred her feet flat on the ground.

"Now, maybe marrying me before I was ready," he said. "That might have been a mistake."

"We did our best, Jonathan."

"But my best wasn't enough. This time I'll make sure. Except there's one problem." He hesitated, looked down. "I'm afraid there's going to have to be a little delay."

"What is it?"

"I need to go to Costa Rica right away. If I don't sign the agreements, I'll lose this partnership and it's crucial."

"When will you leave?"

He grimaced. "Tomorrow." He took her hands again and rubbed her knuckles in a way that kind of hurt. "I'll keep it short. Just four days at the most. Sooner if I can get away. I don't want you to think my heart's not here."

"You have to go. It's a new business."

"Nothing matters more to me than figuring things out between us," he said. "I want to make it right with you."

"It can wait until you get back." She extracted her hands from his scrubbing motion and patted his instead. *I want to make it right with you.*

Not exactly a declaration of passion, but she couldn't offer anything more herself. Worse, the fact that Jonathan would be gone for a few days filled her with relief. He'd come back to her and she wanted him gone?

Just an adjustment.

"Anything I can do to help you succeed, I want to," she said to reassure him.

"Actually…" He played with his flatware. "There is something Belinda suggested."

"What is that?"

"She thinks I should apply for a grant from your foundation. She hit on something really good. To get the word out I need opinion leaders to start a word-of-mouth campaign. If I had funds to sponsor trips for, say college professors, I'd really get a leg up on momentum."

"Sounds interesting," she said.

"Belinda says it's the kind of thing that's right up your alley. But if it puts you in a bad position, I wouldn't even consider—"

"No, no. I think it's great," Esmeralda said.

"Then I'll do it." He grinned. "Belinda offered to help me write the grant. She says she's read tons of them."

"She has. And that's probably a good idea. It'll give her more confidence." And keep her too busy to offer to wash Esmeralda's car or pick up her dry cleaning. It would be a help for Jonathan, too.

Back at the foundation, Esmeralda escaped to her office, her head still pounding, leaving Belinda to go over the grant form with Jonathan.

Her stomach was heavy with sadness and her throat chakra felt as if she'd swallowed a golf ball. She had something she should say. A feeling she'd swallowed. Peppermint tea wasn't going to help. She was relieved Jonathan would be gone, and she missed Mitch like crazy. It was all wrong and she didn't know how to fix it.

ON MONDAY MORNING, three days after her lunch with Jonathan, Esmeralda stood at Belinda's desk waiting for her to get off the phone.

Belinda was turned away, completely intent on the call. "I think that's fabulous," she was saying, her voice more bubbly than usual. "Truly… No, *you* have the good ideas… No, you— Seriously, it's just because I've read so many of them…. No, you can't pay me for the Web site. Absolutely not. Helping you is helping Esmeralda. I mean it." She giggled. "You're making my head swell. When you get back we can go over what I've drafted…. When? Will you be rested tomorrow? Maybe tomorrow night, when Esmeralda has her workshop? Great. I'll set up a presentation, as if you were my client. See you then." She sighed, hung up the phone, then turned in her chair. "Oh! Hi! That was Jonathan," she said. Her face was bright pink. "He's arriving late tonight."

"I know," she said. Jonathan had called her every day to keep her posted on his progress. They planned to see each other on Wednesday night.

"I suggested that I show him the draft of the grant

tomorrow night. Since you have your workshop. Sound okay?"

"It sounds great." Working on the grant seemed to have boosted Belinda's confidence a lot. She seemed less eager for Esmeralda's attention. She seemed...bubblier.

"And I'll need the new financials before my meeting with Mitch at noon," she said.

"Oh. Sure. I'll, um, get on that." Belinda's face went from a cheerful pink to school-paste pale.

"Is there a problem, Belinda?"

"No, no. It's just that Rico is still looking over last month's spreadsheet." She gnawed at her lip.

Something was wrong. And it couldn't be more inconvenient. Esmie didn't want to tell Mitch she couldn't give him what he needed. "So give me what you have. It'll have to do."

"I'll talk to Rico. I'll fix it. Don't worry."

Esmie wouldn't. She had too much else on her mind. In a few hours she'd sit down with Mitch and the draft plan. He'd worked on it over the weekend, he'd told her, and she could tell he wanted her out of his hair. It had only been four days since they'd parted.

When Belinda buzzed her to say Mitch was there, her heart turned over in her chest. "Send him in," she said.

He stopped at the sight of her. "Esmeralda," he said. He'd missed her, she could see it in his eyes.

"How have you been?" she asked.

"Good. Good." He stared at her as if they'd been apart for months, not days.

"Me, too. Good." She didn't know what to do with her hands. She was hot with embarrassment.

"So, shall we get to it?" He cleared his throat and his

eyebrow dipped. "I have a lot to go over with you and I need you to—"

"Fill in some blanks, right. Yeah. You said that."

"I'm repeating myself, huh?" He laughed. "I don't know why I'm so nervous." He gave a rueful smile.

"I do. Things are strained between us."

"But we can do this, can't we? Work together."

"Absolutely," she said, trying to ignore how her body shook with him so near. This was important. Her success was on the line. She'd prepared for this meeting, between nail and palm clients, reading the business-planning book Belinda had brought in. "I have the financials, and I jotted down a few notes of my own."

"Great," he said, then went to sit at her table, opening the portfolio he had prepared.

She sat nearby, aware of his smell, his skin, the way his collar touched his hair. She felt woozy, but fought it. This was important.

"You can see the sections here." He pointed out the tabs for Executive Summary, Market Analysis, Marketing Strategy, Operational Strategy, Critical Risks, Budget, Financials, Promotional Plan, Cost Benefit Analysis and the Appendix, then explained each one in detail.

She was pleased that her study had prepared her to easily grasp what he was showing her. She absorbed the information like a thirsty plant. It was vital to her success, and that prepared her to learn quickly.

"This looks great," she said, "but I'd like to put a Gantt chart in for this first grant cycle."

He lifted his eyebrows. "I'm impressed you know about Gantt charts. It would be useful, I think, but complex to build."

The bar chart would show a timeline for where and how grants would be funded and cycle into contributions. "I think it would show the board how organized we are and it will keep Belinda and me on track as well. I think it's worth it, don't you?"

When he didn't answer, she turned and saw he was inhaling deeply, his eyes closed. "Mitch?" She grinned.

"Huh? Oh. Sorry. It's how you smell. I can't get it out of my head."

"Me, either. About you." They breathed shaky breaths together. "This is hard for me," she said softly.

"Me, too. But we can do it, right?"

"Right," she said and focused in on the next section. "What do you think about a SWOT analysis? I think the board would like that."

"Strengths, weaknesses, opportunities and threats, right? I've seen that done. How do you see it?"

She sketched out the analysis and listed the items she thought of first. Mitch added a few. Then she finished up.

"Looks good," he said, then surveyed her. "You sure as hell did your homework."

"Of course I did. I'm not an idiot."

"I know you're not, Esmie. I was harsh, I know."

"And I was uncertain. It was both of us."

"You're remarkable, you know that?" He looked at her with open admiration.

She blushed. "Let's see how the board meeting goes, huh?" She asked him about the capital growth component, suggesting inviting grant recipients to contribute to the fund. Mitch agreed and pointed out the tax benefits to that move, and before long they were wrapping up.

"Thanks, Mitch," she said, closing the folder. "If you refine this as indicated, I'll get the Gantt chart put together—"

"And you can start working on your presentation next week."

"Sounds good."

"I think the board will be impressed. If you have any questions, let me know."

"I will," she said. Their eyes met. She felt something new, something more than the usual attraction. "Did you notice we didn't argue once?" she said.

"I noticed." He smiled wryly. "I guess it was because we had a clearly defined goal, clearly defined tasks—"

"And it's nice to see you," she said. The fact they'd worked together so well only made things worse.

"So…" He blew out a breath, then looked at his watch. "I better get back to it."

"Yeah. Me, too."

"So, how's that going?" Mitch turned bright red. "With your ex, I mean."

"We've had to put things on hold. Jonathan's been on an urgent business trip. He gets back tonight."

"He left you? 'Hello, I must be going'?"

"He's starting a business, and he had a crucial meeting. I told him to go. We have time."

"If I'd come back I'd never leave your side," he said, practically growling the words. Arousal hummed through her. Mitch would hang on to her the way he held her hand, like he meant business.

"But he's not you," she said, needing to defend Jonathan.

"You got that right." He looked as if he wanted to

say more, do more. Touch her, kiss her, something. He blew out a frustrated breath. "I gotta get out of here." He paused before leaving, turned to her and lifted both her straps from her arms to her shoulders. He patted them in place and sighed. "I hope to hell the guy appreciates you."

He left then, his gait slow, almost reluctant. His energy hovered around her long after he left. She could feel his strength, the power in his eyes, his desire for her, his fingertips lifting her straps.

She hugged herself, shivering.

This wasn't fair to Jonathan. They hadn't even begun to be together. From now on, she had to stay clear of Mitch. He aroused her too much. He could drop off the final report, talk through the details on the phone. She couldn't stand another visit. She would fold, fall into his arms, give up for good.

WHEN MITCH SWUNG HOME Tuesday at noon to get some files he'd left there, he was startled to find Dale working at the kitchen table, papers spread, laptop fired up. Dale rarely rolled out of bed before three. "What's up?" he asked.

"You're here. Great." Dale said. "Take a look at what I've got. You're coming to the workshop tonight, right?"

"To the workshop?" He realized Dale meant the Dream workshop. A week had passed since he and Esmeralda had made love in her plastic pool. It seemed a lifetime ago.

Seeing her yesterday had killed him. He wasn't about to endure that misery again. He'd been impressed by her grasp of the plan, what she'd added, the depth of her knowledge. She was so smart. Too bad she got side-tracked with all that mystical nonsense. She didn't give herself enough credit.

He pulled up a chair and looked through what his brother had written. "You've done a lot of work here."

"Don't sound so surprised." Dale grinned. "I have to get everything organized for Annika tonight. I'm really liking her art therapy thing. I watched her run a session at a domestic abuse center. She's amazing. The kids really get into it."

"I hope this works out for you," Mitch said.

"Don't worry about it, bro," Dale said, putting a hand on his shoulder, as if in comfort. "We put it out into the universe and see what clicks. You get too overwrought about this stuff."

Lord. Dale hadn't even been to a workshop, and he was spouting woo-woo. Must be Annika.

"Just come to the workshop, Mitch."

"I'll try." Now they'd reversed roles.

Dale calmly went back to work, as if this complete change in him was no big deal.

Emotion welled in Mitch. Relief, pleasure, hope and…gratitude. To Esmeralda for making this happen. She'd connected with Dale, brought Annika into the picture to ensure success. Mitch had to thank her.

He'd sworn not to see her again, but he didn't want to thank her over the phone. He couldn't handle the workshop. What if her ex showed up? He'd stop by her office. Easy.

He had to stop letting Mr. Dimples bother him. He and Esmeralda had had great sex. No point in getting greedy. They were too different to take it much further anyway.

Still, whenever he thought of her, he felt like a volcanic river coursed through his veins, sending burning rock to splash and sting him everywhere, making him break out in a sweat, making him shake.

The problem was that it had been so short. Like smelling a freshly baked peach pie, then watching the waitress carry it to someone else's table. Every second you didn't taste it, the pie got more flaky, more juicy. The pie not eaten assumed mythic stature, made your mouth water with soul-deep craving.

Later, back at the office when Maggie buzzed in that Craig was on the line, Mitch was startled. He'd almost forgotten his week-ago call for information. Working with Esmeralda, knowing how sincere she was, he'd put his suspicions on hold.

He punched the button. "Hey, buddy. What's up?"

"It's about your foundation. I hope your brother's not too deep into this."

"What do you mean?" He sat up straighter.

"Remember that bust in that yarn shop and photography studio a couple years ago?"

"Vaguely."

"I'll e-mail the clip. It was big, and it was the Sylvestri crime family. Darien Sylvestri is the ring leader. He's behind bars, but his brothers, Louis and Enzo, are not. Neither is his sister, Olivia Sylvestri Rasbergen, though she's never been linked to any criminal activity. You getting the picture here?"

Dread filled him. "I'm beginning to." Esmeralda trusted Olivia, hadn't looked into anything, didn't even know where the woman's money came from.

"We think the foundation might be set up to launder money," Craig said.

"Interesting. So what's the plan?" His mind raced. Whatever happened, he had to protect Esmeralda. That fact shot through him like lightning. Her only guilt was naiveté. He was kind of pissed at her, though, for getting mixed up in it. If she was so damn psychic, why hadn't she sensed this?

"That's where you come in, Mitch. We could use your help. What's your status with the foundation director? You know her, right?"

"Yes, I do." He took a deep breath. There was no point in denying what he was doing. It was always better to operate in the full light of truth. "I've been working on a business plan for the foundation. As a favor to her."

Craig was silent, reading between the lines.

"We're…friends. And she's innocent of any criminal activity. She's so naive it's almost scary."

"I see. Maybe that's why the Sylvestris are using her. Because she's gullible." But he could feel Craig withhold judgment, not sure of Mitch's loyalties. "The good news is you're in the perfect position to help us without setting off any alarms. You're working on the business plan, so you can ask for financial records, tax returns and all the grants they've purportedly funded."

"I see what you mean." Gloom descended like a curtain.

"You can get the data we need without making a ripple. We can follow every tentacle of the octopus."

"And you're looking for…?"

"Minimum, enough for a grand jury indictment. Maybe a direct prosecution. This could be big, Mitch. The A.G. is very, very interested."

Mitch fought mixed reactions. If there was crime at play, he wanted to help. But if the dirt splashed onto

Esmeralda, he couldn't live with himself. "Wouldn't it be better to enlist Esmeralda's help? I'm sure she'd cooperate."

"Absolutely not. We can't risk her tipping anyone off, even in a misguided attempt to help. Any whiff of suspicion, and they'll bust out and start over somewhere else."

Mitch got Craig's subtext. Mitch could be misguided. Esmeralda could be involved. Craig would need evidence to be sure. Mitch would take the same approach in his place.

Conflict churned inside him.

"If she's innocent it will be obvious, Mitch," Craig said to soothe him. "Truth trumps lies every time. You know how we operate." The department had a reputation for fairness and the pursuit of justice, despite political pressures, Mitch knew. And he certainly didn't want to damage the case by his own interference. Still, he would protect Esmeralda no matter what.

"What if they won't give me the information?"

"Find a way." He meant snoop around, make copies.

"I'm no spy."

"You know how this goes. Once we put things in motion, word gets out. The crooks shred docs, pile on fake paper. We want a surgical strike, not a dragged-out paper chase. You can help us and help your friend, too."

"So, this is for her own good?" he said sarcastically.

"Protect her from the inside."

Craig was right. He wished like hell he wasn't involved, but he was and now he had to use that to his advantage.

"We don't forget our friends, Mitch."

"I'm not interested in currying favor. My work speaks for itself."

"I know that. Just trying to sweeten the poison. I know you didn't ask for this. I'm sorry I'm putting you on the spot."

"It's your job." If the foundation was dirty, Mitch would get Esmeralda out of there as quickly and quietly as possible. He could control the process, limit the hunting expedition.

"I'll do it," he said finally, "as long as you promise me a heads-up on any planned action."

"Whatever I know, you'll know. But I can't be everywhere."

He knew that was true. "Do what you can for me."

"It could turn out to be nothing. Criminals can get religion, right? Maybe it's all as innocent as you think your friend is. You're in the best position to find out."

That, also, was true.

Craig promised to e-mail the news clippings about the Sylvestris, and they hung up.

Damn. Fifteen minutes ago, Mitch had planned to visit Esmeralda to thank her for her help. Now he was going to investigate her.

When he'd first walked in on her, catching her with her feet in the air, he'd had the feeling he was in for trouble.

He just hadn't known what kind or how bad.

10

MITCH GAVE BELINDA TIME TO reach the parking lot before he went to work on her computer. He'd been lucky she was leaving early. Esmeralda was not to be disturbed until five, she'd informed him with a prim sniff. He had twenty minutes.

No pass code required, so he was into her files in seconds. He slid his key drive into a port and copied the accounting spreadsheets and a few other docs that might be of interest. He comforted himself with the fact that Esmeralda would have handed everything over if he could have told her what was up.

Belinda had given him the tax records without complaint. She'd groused about the grant files—making him promise not to lose or mix up any of them—but she'd turned pale when he asked for more current financial records and insisted he wait.

Could she be involved in cooking the books? He hoped not. She seemed eager to please and devoted to Esmeralda.

The news clips from Craig had convinced him something dangerous might be going on. For one thing, what Esmeralda had called a "PR problem" for Duke Dunmore, the strip club owner applying for one of her grants, turned out to be a drug bust involving the Sylvestris. It was all too criminally cozy for his comfort. Mitch would do his part to stop it and protect Esmeralda at the same time.

Finished with the computer, he looked through Belinda's drawers and files, and copied a printout of a marked-up and corrected spreadsheet. If Esmeralda appeared, he planned to tell her Belinda had given him the stuff to copy.

She didn't show, so when he was finished, he headed for her office carrying the file box of grants Belinda had loaned him. Despite his mission, the thought of seeing Esmeralda gave him a rush of heat and hope.

Would she be lying behind her desk, legs in the air again? He didn't smell incense and there was no sitar music behind the door. He braced the file box on his hip and tapped.

"I'm fine, Belinda," she called impatiently. "I don't need smudging or filing or—"

He opened the door. "It's not Belinda."

"Mitch!" She jumped up from her desk, delight lighting her face like sun after rain. "Why are you here? What's that?" She nodded at the file box.

"I wanted to read over all the grants you've funded to maybe include highlights for the plan appendix," he said, wincing internally at the lie. He set the box on her desk.

"That's very thorough of you." She looked him over with those luminous eyes, and he felt guilty as hell.

This was ultimately for her good, he reminded himself. And then he was only aware of her standing so near, watching her chest rise and fall with each breath, taking in the impossible fragility of her collar bones. The river of magma bubbled along his bloodstream again.

"I also wanted to thank you. Dale's working on the grant with Annika. I've never seen him so motivated. You made that happen."

"We did it together—both of us."

"I'd have blown it without you. You let Dale figure it out. I would have shoved. You coaxed. You did this."

"I'm glad I could help."

"He's coming to the workshop tonight. He wanted me to come, but I didn't think it would be a good idea."

"No? I guess you're right." She sighed so sadly.

"So he's back?" he mumbled, feeling like an idiot. It was none of his business. "You've seen him?"

"Not yet. Tomorrow night."

"I see." How could the guy wait? What a loser. But then he'd brought her dead daisies. Esmeralda grew her own daisies. If you wanted to give her something, you got exotic fruit or fancy tea or, hell, one of those polished stones she had all over the place.

"I'm a little nervous actually. It's been six years, and we've both changed." Her eyes would not stay on his face and she was biting her lip again.

She was so loyal, she'd give Mr. Dimples and his bad gifts chance after chance.

He felt a terrible mix of guilt about the data in his pocket, a fierce drive to protect her at all costs, jealousy of her clueless ex and an aching need to take her into his arms.

He could not walk away. He felt the way he had under that meteor shower in her play pool, when they'd first made love—that this was inevitable, unstoppable, that forces beyond his control were at work.

As if she'd read his mind, she lifted her eyes, which,

until that moment, had darted everywhere but his face, and met his gaze straight on.

"We need more time," he said. "We're not done."

"What about Jonathan?" she said, her voice shaking.

"What about us?" There it was, what he felt. He wanted a chance with her.

"Oh, Mitch," she said, surrendering. She grabbed his shirt like a drowning woman going for the last life boat and yanked him close, putting her tongue deep in his mouth, squirming against him, as though she wanted to climb into him.

He walked her to her sofa. She'd barely landed in its soft grip when he had her blouse up, her bra unlatched and his hands on the soft flesh of her breasts.

"When you touch me I can't think," she said. "I can only feel. I can't even...I lose all...oh..."

He put his mouth on her breast and reached under the yards of skirt to touch her beneath her panties. She squirmed, alive under his finger. "Get inside me," she moaned. "And whatever you do, don't stop."

He freed himself, shoved her skirt up and her panties down and entered her. She was slick and swollen and he reached deep.

"So good. Don't stop. Don't ever stop." She sounded as desperate as he felt. They were the same suddenly, united by the experience of this abrupt, all-encompassing heat. It was like a monsoon storm that blew over trash bins, whipped palm trees into a froth, sent stoplights swinging, drove rain in blinding sheets, unstoppable, not taking no for an answer.

Right now, Esmeralda was saying *yes* over and over, moaning it low and crying it high, and he thrust in and out again and again, heedless of everything but the driving need to get there.

They were in her office, the door wasn't even locked, but he didn't care. They could have been on the burning asphalt in a parking lot, in the backseat of his Lexus, or on a bed at the Valley Ho, it was all the same to him. He just had to have her, the strawberry-orange smell of her, her mouth on his, her soft cries in his ears, their need as rhythmic as the thrusts of his cock. He couldn't get enough of her body, of her. It was like a sickness, a sweet plague.

He thrust in hard. Maybe too hard. "Are you okay?"

"I'm good. Great…keep…doing…that… Don't stop." She clung to him, her ankles locked around his ass, holding on, as if as long as he stayed inside her she wouldn't have to think about anything else. That's how he felt, for sure.

Her cries were now mewling and desperate, coming faster. "Mitch…I'm…I'm…"

"You're coming." He felt her sex close around him, squeezing him as she climaxed. He held himself back, wanting to feel every twitch and spasm of her release, wanting her to feel safe in his arms while she flew. He felt her entire body vibrate with pleasure.

When her movements slowed, he let go himself, holding onto her, keeping her safe. They breathed together for a few seconds, gradually slowing down, while reality, with its unfortunate truths, settled around them like a gray cloud.

The woman wanted to be with her ex-husband. Mitch was investigating her company. Instead of accepting those two truths, he'd blurted, "What about us?" and thrown her onto her sofa. So out of control. So not like him.

"Oh, dear," Esmeralda moaned, obviously feeling regrets, too. Then her shoulders shook, and he realized she was crying. He'd made her cry. And he thought Mr. Dimples was an ass.

He wrapped his arms around her. "I'm sorry. That was my fault."

"No, it wasn't. I can't stop wanting you. I don't know what to do. This is so unfair to Jonathan."

He patted her back, not sure what to say that would help.

She pulled away and looked at him, her face full of anguish. "I'm so confused. When you showed up, I was expecting him, but maybe it was supposed to be you. Then he came…."

"What are you talking about?"

"There was a prediction," she said miserably, closing her bra and pulling down her top. "I had some readings done for my thirty-fifth birthday—the fifth lunar cycle is big—and all three said I was supposed to begin anew with a man from my past. Exactly those words. Even Belinda, who's barely learning to read tarot, picked up on it."

"Okay…"

"I expected Jonathan because of how abruptly we divorced and how close we were. But then you showed up on our anniversary, and there was the meteor shower—"

"You thought I showed up because of a prediction?"

She nodded. "Three of them."

He felt queasy.

"I know you don't believe in any of this, Mitch. Which is why I didn't tell you before, but now I don't know what to do. Jonathan came back, but I have this *thing* for you."

"You make it sound like a disease."

"It clearly interferes with how I feel about Jonathan."

Count your blessings. He had the sense not to say that out loud. He wasn't sure what would become of him and Esmeralda, he just knew they needed time to find out.

"I told Jonathan we would try, but I did this." She motioned at him. "I have no honor whatsoever." She buried her face in his shirt and he patted her awkwardly, hoping that helped. He wanted to do something tangible. Make a call, arrange a settlement, pay a bill, get a second opinion, change the damn tire. *Something* besides just sit by, going *there-there* in the face of her pain.

That seemed to be what she wanted, however. After a few minutes, she took a shuddering breath, then pushed away from his arms. "I have to tell Jonathan what happened." She squared her shoulders, determined.

"Does he know about me?"

"I told him that I was seeing someone, but that it wasn't serious." She looked at him. *Is it serious?*

It felt serious. But he'd always kept it light with women, so what did he know? He felt tongue-tied, and his brain hissed with white noise. "What are you going to tell him?"

"I don't know." Her shoulders sagged. "It's not like I know what's going to happen with you and me. We've basically only argued and had sex."

"And worked together. The business plan, remember?"

She shrugged as though that wasn't much to go on. "It's been frantic…coupling, really. An obsession."

She had a point.

Her eyes burned into him. "I mean, you and I hardly

know each other and what we do know we don't very much like."

"That's not entirely true." Though the idea that she thought fate had a hand in their meeting was a perfect example of how different they were.

"This could just be physical—you and me—and that's not fair to Jonathan." She put a finger to her lip, pondering it.

Forget Jon Boy. He had his chance. I was here first. Primitive and childish thoughts, but he wasn't thrilled with her line of thinking, either.

"There's only one thing to do." Her chin jutted up.

"What's that?" he asked. *Forget him and be with me.*

"I just can't sleep with anyone."

"You can't? How does that help?" Gloom filled him. He definitely didn't like this line of thinking.

"Having sex with you could be my way of hiding from my true feelings, from what I really need in my life."

"You mean…him? You think you need him?" *Ouch.* That made Mitch what? Stand-in stud? Jealousy shot through him.

"I have to find out. Sex colors too much."

And makes it all worthwhile. But he just sighed. "So you're going to tell him that?" At least Jon Boy wouldn't be sleeping with her either. Somehow that assuaged Mitch's caveman ego.

"Yes. When I see him in person, I think." She looked at her watch. "I've got the workshop tonight. So, that's settled, I guess." She sighed and leaned against him, fitting snugly, curved in all the right places. She rested a hand on his thigh. Her breathing slowed, deepened, got raspy. So did his. Her hand moved a little, and he went hard as a rock.

"Esmie," he breathed into the hair near her ear.

"I should leave." She pushed to her feet, as though she'd escaped from quicksand, and headed for the door.

"Uh, I believe this is your office? Maybe I'm the one who should leave?" He grinned.

"That's right. You leave." She pulled open the door.

He went to her and touched her cheek. "You sure about this no sex thing?"

"Positive," she said, but she bit her lip so he knew it wouldn't be any easier for her. "Maybe you should come tonight. For Dale? And to see how everyone's doing? Aren't you curious?"

"I can help you set up." Who was he kidding? He just wanted to be with her a little longer.

11

ESMERALDA WATCHED MITCH give the monster sofa one last shove into place, and sighed. "That's it, I guess."

She'd been alone with Mitch for only a few minutes while they cleaned up, but the time had been electric, an endless stream of sparks and tingles and urges. "Thanks so much."

But instead of moving for the door, Mitch dropped onto the sofa, which made her feel guiltily pleased. She sat beside him, not close, but not far enough away, since her skin still prickled and attraction beat between them, steady as a pulse.

It was wrong to tempt herself. She'd made a sensible decision. No sex. But she craved him more every second.

Mitch drummed his fingers on the arm of the sofa. Those fingers…mmm… They knew her body's every spot. Just thinking about those digits made her so achy she needed a pain reliever.

And she knew exactly which one. "Uh, I'm getting ice water," she said, lurching to her feet. "Want some?" *To pour over us?*

"Sounds good."

She left Mitch petting the dogs, who adored him. *What are you doing?* She had no idea. Obsessively wanting someone couldn't be good, but neither was not wanting them at all, which was how she felt about Jonathan.

So far. That was the point. Maybe all she needed was distance from Mitch and time with Jonathan. But now Mitch was in her living room, and she was glad.

Who knew what Mitch really felt for her? He could be just jealous, an elk bashing the moss off his horns in a duel with a rival buck. He sure hadn't declared eternal devotion.

But then neither had she.

She filled two glasses with water and started back. What was her true fate? Was she on the right path or lying in the ditch? She was blind and deaf to any psychic vibe.

She knew she needed help if she was ever to get her head above this sea of hormones, doubt and guilt, so she'd done the smartest thing. She'd called her mentor Lenore for a reading.

Well, left her a message, since Lenore was constantly away at conferences and retreats. A phone consult would do. Lenore was the solution to this problem for sure.

She handed a glass to Mitch and sat beside him. "So, Dale and Annika's grant looks good, don't you think?" Talking was the only excuse they had for spending more time together.

"Yeah. Dale showed me a side of him I've never seen before. Serious, responsible and smart. I'm thinking that if they get the grant I'll volunteer to work with the kids."

"I bet you'll enjoy that. Are you playing again?"

"I'm considering it. Ever since that night at the supper club, I guess."

"I'm glad. You were always so good. I can't picture you without music in your life."

"I'm different around you. Lighter. You make me laugh at myself. And that's something every lawyer needs."

"We could start a movement. Laughs for Lawyers."

"Yucking it up in court? I don't know. There's nothing funny about a tort, young lady."

She laughed. She liked being with him like this, just enjoying each other's company.

The phone rang. She started to rise.

"Let your machine get it," he said. "Be with me."

She stayed. Why not? Be in the moment. With Mitch. She smiled at him, feeling funny listening to her message kick in, as if she was playing hooky. Her message ended with "Love and light," then the beep sounded.

"Esmie, it's Jonathan."

"Oh." She looked at Mitch.

"You'd better pick up," he said.

She lunged for the phone, feeling funny with Mitch on her couch. "Hi," she said, turning away from Mitch.

"You were screening?" Jonathan asked. "You never screen."

"Sorry," she said "We just finished with the workshop."

"How did it go?"

"Great. Quite successful. Everyone's making progress."

"Glad to hear it. I met with Belinda about my grant. She's a wonder." He paused. "Really has a way with words." He paused again. He seemed to need to build up to say something.

Which was exactly her problem. How should she put it? *I'm obsessed with Mitch so I can't sleep with either of you?* Jonathan had barely kissed her. Still, she should

give him a clue, let him know there were obstacles.
"Listen, Jonathan, I—"

"Esmie, I hate—"

They laughed at their colliding words.

"You go first," Jonathan said.

"No, no. You called me," she said. "What is it?"

"I'm afraid it's bad news. I have to leave again.
There's a preschool program in Brazil that I very much
want as a project. Believe it or not, I've got competition.
My contact in Costa Rica gave me an introduction, but
I have to make the connection in person. It's really an
issue of relationships and—"

"You have to go. Of course. When do you leave?"

"In the morning at eight. It's a twenty-two-hour
flight. I'm so sorry, Esmie. I'll make it as quick as I can.
But there is so much bureaucracy to deal with. I'm
afraid it will be at least a week. I have to play it by ear."

"This is important. It's your business. I understand."

"You are the most understanding woman in the
world. Thank you. Now what did you want to tell me?"

"It's just that we need to talk." She glanced at Mitch.
"But it can wait until you get back."

"Good. I agree. We do need to talk." He sighed,
almost as if he had a confession of his own. But that was
probably wishful thinking. She dreaded hurting him.

"So we'll talk when you get back?"

"Sounds right."

Probably better. By then she would have consulted
with Lenore, and her path would be clear. They said
goodbye and she turned slowly to Mitch.

"You look upset," he said. "If you really want to talk
to him, I'll leave. It's late anyway. I should go."

"I'm not sure what to say." She felt miserable about it. She sat on the sofa again. "We'll talk when he gets back. It'll be a week at least."

He nodded, then seemed to be thinking something over. "What happened between you two?" he asked. "If you don't mind telling me."

"No. If you really want to hear. We met seven years ago when Jonathan came to me for a reading. We liked each other and connected so strongly. It was like we read each other's minds."

"Really? Like telepathy?"

"Not telepathy. We just were in synch."

"Okay. I get that." He seemed relieved that she wasn't talking about anything psychic.

"After a few months, he asked me to marry him and it felt right." She hadn't even consulted anyone. Jonathan had seemed so sure and she had no issues. When the marriage had failed, her doubts about her own instincts had surfaced and stuck. Were still there, now that she thought about it.

"We only disagreed in one area—finances," she continued. "Jonathan was always more—how do I put it?— *positive* about spending than I was."

"So…he gambled? Put you in debt?" His question seemed protective of her, not critical of Jonathan.

"He invested our savings in a real estate partnership that failed. He read the prospectus a tad too favorably and didn't consult with me."

"That's pretty bad."

"The problem was that I hassled him about money so much I made it impossible for him to talk to me about it."

"I don't buy that."

"You don't know him. He meant well."

He blew out a breath. "Yeah, I guess I understand. I funded a music store for Dale without looking too closely at the market or the capital costs. Dale's pretty optimistic, too."

"We were going to buy a house with the money, and Jonathan felt so guilty that he couldn't face me. He left, then filed divorce papers."

"He just left you? Like that?"

"He wanted me to move on, not be tied down by his mistakes."

"You insist on giving everyone the benefit of the doubt, don't you?"

"I do. And I was right. Jonathan wants to pay me back."

"He should."

"The money doesn't matter to me. What matters is that he has a better attitude about wealth now. He's more realistic. He's figured it all out."

"That's good, I guess." Mitch seemed to be doing his best to give a rival the benefit of the doubt.

"Which is why he deserves another chance. We both do."

There was a moment of silence while Mitch pondered what she'd said. "That all sounds good except for one thing," Mitch said, turning to her. "You're not in love with him."

"I love him. I've always loved him."

He shook his head. "There's no heat. You talk about him like he's a friend, like family, not a man you want to be with."

He'd gotten to the heart of the matter, of course, which was Mitch's way.

"Some things take time, Mitch. I owe him the time."

"Okay," he said, disagreeing, but respecting her enough not to argue. "It's up to you." His dark eyes roiled with emotion. Respect, frustration, jealousy, tenderness and, above all, desire. He wanted her. He wanted what they had. Now.

And she wanted it, too. Despite her story, despite how sensible she'd sounded, she wanted him to pull her into his arms and kiss her mindless.

"I should get out of here," Mitch said, softly, reading her thoughts. "Before this gets out of hand again."

"You should," she agreed shakily.

"It's hard to be this close to you and not be able to touch you." He brushed her strap with a finger, lighting her on fire.

"Don't. I can't…bear it."

His eyes glowed with dark fire. "Neither can I." He headed for the door, pausing to scrub the two dogs' backs in farewell.

She went with him and in the open doorway lifted her gaze to the night sky.

"Looking for a sign?" he asked.

"Maybe," she said with a sigh. "No more falling stars."

"It's so hard to leave you," he said, cupping her cheek.

"I know." She ached for him.

"Hell, maybe my battery will be dead and I'll have to stay." He smiled and backed away.

"Good night," she said, closing the door fast, and resting against it to keep herself from calling him back.

Tonight he'd seemed more like a friend. He'd listened to her story, made decent comments, actually helped her think through her situation a bit. And had an alarming insight about her lack of feeling for Jonathan. Which made things even more complicated.

She pressed her back to the door and felt flames lick her insides. She wanted him so badly. How was she supposed to connect with Jonathan when all she could think of was Mitch?

Maybe she had to sleep with Mitch. Finish with him before she could be with Jonathan. Clear her system of him. Why hadn't she thought of it before? It was perfect. The truth of it raged through her. Of course. She had to go to him. She had to—

The doorbell rang and she nearly jumped out of her skin.

It was Mitch and he looked amazed. "My battery *is* dead. I can't believe it. Summer's hard on batteries, but I just replaced this one and—"

"Get in here!" She yanked him by his shirt into her house and slammed the door and kissed him hard.

He broke off. "What are you doing?"

"This will just get worse," she said, hardly able to form words. "We have to be together."

"Are you sure?" He wrapped his arms around her, kissing her neck, his breath harsh in her ear.

"Completely. Come on." This time they were going to her bedroom, not the play pool, not the painful sofa. This time they were making love on purpose, not by accident. She took his hand and led him to her bedroom.

Together they tugged off clothes in the golden light of her bedside lamp. She pulled back the covers and they laid their grateful bodies on the soft, cool surface.

She loved the warm human length of him, his erection solid against her stomach. She'd said yes, suspended judgment. For once she would trust her instincts, not analyze, evaluate, second-guess.

They clung to each other, as if amazed by their good fortune, like lovers reunited after being separated by war or natural disaster or a misreported death.

She would not let anything keep her from the complete joy of a physical act that seemed like a miracle.

"I want you so much," Mitch said, sounding as mystified as she felt. He bent to kiss her mouth, caress her breasts, kissing each one in turn. He seemed to be memorizing her. "I've never felt like this before."

"Me, either," she said. "Never."

She parted her legs, he shifted over her and entered gently. It was as easy and effortless as sliding into August water, the water silk on the skin, no drag at all.

Their bodies moved in complete harmony. Their minds were another matter, but she would not think of that. She only lifted her hips, taking him deeper, holding on.

She inhaled the scent of his cologne and clean sweat, listened to the rasp of breath, felt the slippery glide of their moist bodies. "You feel so good inside me," she breathed.

"Like I belong," he said, his brown eyes flaring with wonder.

"You do belong." Despite their differences, their disputes, perhaps he was her man. Each lift of her hips and thrust of his cock seemed to make it more true, pulling them closer, making them one in heat and need and connection.

Her sex knotted tighter and tighter, eager for release, but still wanting to prolong the moment, to build the thrill. She arched her breasts upward, inviting his mouth.

He took a nipple in, tugged it, as if to join her even more tightly to him.

His arms held her close, his thighs pressed hers together, telling her he would protect her, pleasure her, be anything she needed him to be.

She felt utterly female, completely carnal, in tune with the universe. He groaned, swept away, and she loved that she affected him so strongly. They moved fast, then faster, stilled, waited and crossed over. As her climax hit, she breathed his name.

"I'm here," he said and joined her in release, shaking with the power of it. She trembled, too, and wrapped her arms around his back, holding on, trying to catch up with herself. Finally, she looked into his eyes. He was here for her, steady and strong.

He fell back on the bed, tucking her against him. "Don't start thinking," he warned. "Thinking won't help us."

She curled into him and tried to obey. But Jonathan came into her mind, accompanied by the oddest thought. *He'll be happy for you.* Wishful thinking at its finest, no doubt. But she refused to let doubts lap at her joy.

Tonight, Mitch was staying. He had no choice. His battery was dead. Whether that was through cosmic intervention or the brutal Arizona sun, she didn't care to know.

12

EARLY THE NEXT MORNING, Mitch woke to find himself wrapped around Esmeralda as if he was afraid she might escape. She wasn't acting as though she would. She was cuddled into the pillows, smiling in her sleep, from what he could see, as if they'd been sleeping together for years and would keep on doing it forever.

Would they?

Last night he'd said he belonged inside her. *Belonged.* The overblown sentiment made him cringe. He'd made it sound somehow metaphysical, as though Esmeralda had rubbed off on him. That was downright weird.

She hadn't blinked an eye, either. She'd agreed with him.

Meanwhile, he was helping the A.G.'s office investigate her. He'd dropped the files and key drive at Craig's on the way to the workshop. Without blinking an eye. And now he'd slept with her. He felt like a traitor.

When Esmeralda learned about it, she'd feel betrayed. On the other hand, if nothing came of the investigation, she might not ever hear. Maybe he was dreaming, but that was easy to do holding her this way.

She felt so good in his arms. He was lying there grinning to himself that very minute. He shifted to study her in sleep. Her face was smooth, worry free, her curls covering one cheek. The sheet outlined her curves, cupping her nipple, sinking in at her waist. She looked like Sleeping Beauty after the prince had done a great deal more than kiss her awake.

Looking at all her lush beauty, he wanted to take her again, bury himself to the hilt, stroke her to cries of pleasure and join her there.

Haven't you had enough? They'd gone at it until late in the night. Today was a work day for both of them. How would they be in the light of day? He wished they were as good together upright as they were lying down. Or on their sides…or sitting…or…

Stop.

Could he possibly be what she needed? Could they work out their differences?

And what about Jon Boy?

For now, he slid gently away, letting her sleep. She rolled his way, feeling for him, so he put a pillow where he'd been. She clutched it against her chest, content.

So cute. His heart lifted. He'd told her that when he was around her he felt better, and it was true. He felt lighter, more at ease with the world. Not that his life weighed him down, but maybe he'd been a tad intense, serious, goal driven. It wouldn't hurt him to loosen up, have more fun.

He went to make coffee. When she got up they would talk. How would that go? He rolled his shoulders, not eager for this little heart-to-heart. Too much was up in the air.

She'd have to jump-start his car or drive him to work.

He could roust Dale if he had to, he guessed. Odd for his battery to quit cold. It was as if he'd willed it so he could be with her.

Clothes in hand, he tiptoed down the hall. The dogs trotted after him, whining. "Shh," he said. "Let her sleep. I'll feed you."

He entered her kitchen, painted bright yellow and sky-blue with a border of daisies up by the ceiling. Sunlight poured through a window onto a cheerful red Buddha surrounded by small candles and live daisies in pots. He liked this room. It felt sunny and serene. Like Esmeralda.

That's afterglow, pal. Wind it down.

He shrugged and got the dog food from the pantry, then went to make coffee. Except there were no beans and no pot. She was a tea drinker. Of course. He found a dozen flavors in the cupboard above the stove, where a sleek red teapot rested on a burner.

Her phone rang. He heard her voice from the bedroom, sleepy, talking to someone. The woman was always on the phone.

He'd just poured the boiling water into two teacups when she spoke near him.

"I make a mean fruit blintz," she said, her voice still fuzzy from sleep. "Sound good?"

"Something quick is fine. Toast." His traitorous belly rumbled loudly.

"Sounds like you'd like something more."

"That my stomach chakra giving me away?"

"Chakra…excellent. You're learning." She beamed at him, reading too much into the remark, but what the hell.

He wrapped her in his arms. "You okay?"

She nodded against his shoulder. "I feel a little funny."

He leaned back to look in her eyes. "Guilty?"

She nodded. "I'll have to call him and tell him what's going on. We can't ignore what's between us, Mitch." She searched his face.

"No. We can't." He handed her a tea cup and sipped some of his. It was hot and sweet. Strawberry Zinger. Of course.

She found the recipe she wanted, propped open the page, and laid out the cooking ingredients and tools.

He set the table, all the while watching her bustle and hum, fighting how much he wanted to just catch all that energy and hold it in his arms. Forget work, forget everything except her.

The phone rang. "Would you wash these?" She handed him pint containers of blueberries and strawberries, then ran to the phone.

He washed the berries and listened to Esmeralda give someone advice about a mother-in-law's visit, a boyfriend and a meditation technique.

She'd barely hung up when the phone rang again. "Sorry," she called to him. "People know to catch me before I leave for work. I'll be right there."

He sighed, read the recipe and whipped up the batter. Blintzes were just crepe burritos, he could see. While the thin pancakes sizzled in oil, he mixed up the filling, adding a couple things he'd picked up from living through Dale's gastronomical tsunamis.

Esmeralda stayed on the phone. They couldn't have had a heart-to-heart about their future if they'd wanted to. It was almost laughable.

The blintzes weren't pretty, but they tasted damn

good, if he did say so himself, and he laid everything on the table, including a small bowl of extra berries for garnish. "Esmeralda! Come on. It's ready."

"Be right there," she called to him.

No way would he let this go cold. He marched to where she stood. "Call back. Breakfast's up."

"Sorry," she mouthed, then finished the call quickly. "She's having trouble quitting smoking," she explained.

"I want you to taste the blintzes you made for me." He led her to the table.

She sat down, her eyes wide. "Wow. What a great job I did."

He fed her a bite, enjoying the way she leaned in, eager, her tongue swirling around the morsel, her lips moist.

God, he wanted her.

She closed her eyes. "Delicious." She smacked her lips, then opened her eyes. "What's that extra flavor?"

"A splash of Amaretto and a little nutmeg."

"All this and you can cook? How lucky I am." She leaned to give him a berry-flavored kiss, and he knew he would never taste a piece of fruit without thinking of her.

He took a bite himself. Not bad. The pastry was delicate, the filling melted on contact and the berries were sweet explosions against his tongue.

"This is fun, huh?" she said with a contented sigh.

"Yeah." He could get used to this, sitting with her in the mornings, feeding each other, grinning between bites, sun splashing the table, the dogs lolling at their feet.

She considered him for a long moment, chin in her palm.

He stopped eating, fork halfway to his mouth. "What?"

"I'm just wondering about you is all. I told you about

Jonathan. What about the women in your life? Have you ever been serious? Engaged?"

"No. I've had girlfriends, but never for too long. There was law school and building my practice and…I don't know." It sounded so lame when he said it out loud. Exactly why had he stayed so isolated? He had to show he had *some* heart.

"There was one woman I wanted to get serious with. Recently." Lord, could he tell her about Julie? She'd barely been a hope. "She was my associate, so it was a bad idea."

"Did you break up? Is she still working for you?"

"Yes. I mean no. I mean she's still working for me, and we didn't break up because we weren't ever together. It was all in my head." He should have been mortified by this confession, but Esmeralda was listening kindly, not judging him, not thinking him a fool.

"How come nothing happened?"

"Like I said, we worked together, but, also, I didn't realize how I felt for a while, but then I did and I wanted to talk to her, but it turned out she was with someone else."

"I'm sorry, Mitch. That must have hurt."

"It was my own fault. I don't know why I held back so long, why I didn't act sooner."

"You had other priorities," she said, clearly trying to give him an out. Her eyes were reading him like a CT scan, not missing anything.

"Yeah, but that's not the whole story. I just want it to be right. I don't want to get invested in something that won't work out. Half of all marriages end in divorce." He shrugged.

"You don't want to get hurt."

"Who does?"

"But you're an intense person under your calm. You tend to guard your feelings, mask your reactions."

She was correct, but he didn't like the way she'd begun to sound as though she was reading his fortune or something. "I want it to be right. The right person, the right time, the right approach."

"You want it to be perfect."

"Who doesn't?" He felt as if she'd lifted the blinds on a comfortably dark corner of his soul, and he was blinking against the brightness.

"I'm that way." She gave a sad smile. "But maybe nothing's perfect. Maybe you just work with what comes your way." She held his gaze, not letting go. Was that what they were going to do?

When her phone rang this time, he was relieved. A little self-analysis went a long way. "I'll do the dishes," he said as she took off for the phone.

He was surprised to realize he felt okay…better. The way it felt to pry out a sliver. The digging around hurt like hell, but the relief was heaven.

When she returned, they started making out at the sink. He was just about to drag her back to bed for a quickie when the phone rang again. "Leave it," he said, kissing her more deeply.

"I'm expecting an important call." She pried herself out of his arms, surprisingly determined.

"Was that it?" he asked when she returned.

She shook her head and rubbed herself against him. "Now where were we?"

"What could be more important than this?" He nuzzled her neck, squeezed her ass until she squirmed against him.

"It's Lenore," she murmured. "I asked her for a reading."

"A reading?" He cupped her breast, slid his hand down to stroke her, teasing a little.

"I need help figuring out what to do about us and about Jonathan," she breathed, getting into what he was doing.

What? He stopped kissing her and pulled back. "You're asking a palm reader what to do about us?"

"To help me clarify and decide the right path."

"You're handing your life over to some psychic?"

"Lenore's not *some psychic*. She's exceptionally talented. She has clients around the world. And she knows me very well." She steadied her gaze on him. "Please try to control your disdain."

"Sorry." He didn't mean to be harsh, but the last thing he needed was to be reminded of her kooky beliefs. "This is complicated enough as it is, without all that…" *Crazy stuff.* He had the sense not to say it.

"There are forces beyond us that we can learn from. We have to be humble and open and trusting."

"Trust yourself, Esmeralda. Trust me. This is between us."

"This is who I am, Mitch."

"Look, I'm trying to be tolerant about your beliefs, but I don't share them and I sure won't make life decisions based on superstitious mumbo-jumbo."

She sucked in a breath, and her eyes filled with hurt that swirled into anger. "I didn't realize how little respect you have for me," she said slowly, her voice low.

"I respect you, Esmeralda. I just don't believe what you believe. That's not a character flaw. It's normal."

"And I'm not? You think I'm nuts? You do. Not quite

right in the head." She blew out a breath. "I don't know what to say."

"I don't think you're crazy. That's not it. But you have to admit your ideas are unusual."

"Just because you can't accept anything beyond what you can see or sense or prove, doesn't mean it isn't there, Mitch. I happen to—"

The phone rang again.

"Does it ever stop?"

"No, it doesn't," she snapped.

"Set some limits, Esmeralda. I've never been here when you haven't had a half-dozen intrusive calls."

"I don't consider them intrusive. They're gifts. It's an honor to help people. If you can't accept that, then you don't accept me." Her eyes flashed blue-green fire, and she marched off to take the call.

He stomped off to shower and dress. *Hell.* One minute they were rubbing each other into a frenzy and the next they were ripping each other a new one.

She got pissed at him so fast. That wasn't like her. She was a calm, cheerful person around everyone else. Only he made her edgy and defensive. She did the same to him. He prided himself on his cool head, but a few disagreeable words with her and the next thing he knew he turned into an arrogant, judgmental ass.

By the time she got off the phone, he was ready to go. He had a meeting to get to, so he asked her for a jump and they headed for her carport in awkward silence.

He climbed into his car. "I'll give it a try first."

She stood beside his open window, looking sexy and tousled and sad. His fault. He'd make it up to her somehow.

He turned the key and the engine started instantly. He couldn't believe it. "It was dead last night. I swear."

"Maybe it *was* a sign." She smiled.

He loved her smile, the way it filled her face, and how quick she was to be kind, the way her eyes wouldn't let go, even when they saw more than he meant to show.

"Maybe it was," he said. He put his hand over hers on the window ledge. "We'll figure it out together, Esmie. Somehow."

Holding her hand, looking into her face, he knew he wasn't giving up without a fight.

He didn't care what any palm reader said to her.

ESMERALDA WATCHED MITCH GO, happy and miserable at once. How could they be meant to be together? What lesson could they possibly have for each other? Patience? Tolerance? The importance of sex?

That, for sure. She could still feel his arms around her. Memories of their lovemaking brushed her body like a gossamer shawl, sending shocks and prickles and shivers across her skin, down her spine, across her scalp and to the tips of her toes.

Everything else was all wrong. Well, not everything. But they got on each other's nerves so easily.

What to do, what to do? *Lenore, please call.*

In the meantime, Jonathan had to know. She'd violated her no-sex plan before she'd even told the man about it. Poor Jonathan. He would be so hurt. She looked at her watch. He'd be at the airport still, she thought, and dialed his cell.

"What's wrong?" he asked as soon as he heard her voice.

"Can you talk for a minute?"

"For a bit. I'm in line at security. Are you all right, Esmie?"

"I'm fine. Miserable, but fine."

"What's made you miserable?"

"It's Mitch. I've been seeing Mitch."

He sucked in a breath. Then she heard the strangest thing. His exhale sounded like a *Whew*. He was relieved? Maybe that it wasn't anything worse.

"You told me there was someone else," he said calmly. "Your feelings can't disappear instantly."

"But I told you it wasn't serious. I don't know that it is, but it's just not…going away." She swallowed the knot in her throat. *I'm falling in love with him.* She couldn't say that. She didn't want to even think it.

"There's one other thing you should know, Jonathan. See, I knew him from before. We barely met, but when he came back, I thought…" Her throat was so tight she could hardly squeeze out the words.

"That he was the man from your past. Of course. That makes sense." He sounded oddly calm, almost cheerful. "Things happen for a reason, Esmie."

"You think so?"

"Sure. You do, too."

"I don't know what I believe anymore." Since Mitch had walked in her door, she'd doubted herself—her impulses, her gifts, her ability to run the foundation.

"I have complete confidence in you. You know that."

"I do." Jonathan's confidence in her was automatic. He handed out compliments like jelly beans. Mitch wasn't like that. Which was why his praise when they worked on the business plan had meant so much….

Stop comparing them.

"Gotta go," Jonathan said. "I'm at the checkpoint. I'll call from Brazil when I can. We'll talk it all out when I get back. All of it. Just don't worry."

She told him goodbye. He'd been remarkably calm, even about the fact that Mitch might be the man who'd been predicted to return to her life. Maybe he was in shock.

Her phone rang, interrupting her analysis. "Hello?"

"Hey, Esmie." It was Jill. "Listen, tonight's the night. Lindy wants to pick up Huffington. Probably Pistol, too. Thanks for hanging on to them for me."

"Tonight? Oh. I see." Tears stung her eyes. "It was a joy to have them." Her voice shook. Not tonight. She couldn't bear it. Huffington whined up at her and Pistol did an anxious spin around her legs. The dogs *knew*. At least Mitch wasn't here to make her feel stupid for believing dogs could be psychic, too.

WHEN SHE GOT TO WORK, Belinda waylaid her before she could even make some tea. "Could you read this grant, Esmeralda?" Belinda asked anxiously. "It's what I drafted for Jonathan, and I'd love your feedback."

So weary and worried she thought her brain might pop, she nevertheless sat beside Belinda's desk and began to read. In a few moments, she raised her eyes. "You wrote this?"

Belinda nodded, her earrings jingling softly. "Is it okay?"

"It's great. It's thorough, concise, persuasive and well researched. And the idea is great. This is a yes, no question."

"Oh, thank you!" Belinda leaned over and hugged her hard. "Jonathan will be so happy. I'll call him and tell him once he lands in Brazil. Unless you want to."

"I'm sure he'd be glad to hear the news from you."

"You know, my fingers just flew writing it. I just opened my heart and it flowed out. The keyboard was burning. It was so easy I figured I was missing something."

"When you're good at something it does seem easy."

Belinda sighed. "Thanks for giving me the chance to shine."

"That's my job. And you're doing great." With the grants Belinda had penciled a "yes" on, they hovered at twenty-five approvals. "I think you should come to the workshops. You can help people draft their grants. How would that be?"

"Really? Oh. I would love that. Thank you so much. For your faith in me…it means so much." Then her face sagged and her eyes danced away.

"What's wrong?" *Pay attention to this.* The impulse came with a surge of heat down Esmie's spine. A premonition.

"It's that, well, I'm still a little confused about the books. Rico's not good at explaining them."

Address this. Dig in.

But her mind was already overcrowded with worry. She had just two weeks and two days before the board meeting. If she kept with her schedule, no slack, she could make the fifty-grant goal. She still had her presentation to prepare when Mitch finalized the plan. Her dogs were leaving tonight. What about Mitch? What about Jonathan?

Some problems took care of themselves. She needed

to buoy Belinda's confidence, didn't she? Make up for all the past doubts? "I have faith in you," she said.

"Okay," Belinda said with an uncertain sigh. "You sound like Jonathan. He trusted me with his grant. He's a good man."

"He is." And he'd grown since the divorce. So why did Esmie feel only gentle friendliness toward him? Was she resisting her fate by clinging to her attraction to Mitch?

"Thanks to him I know the kind of man I want in my life." Belinda suddenly went pink. "No more players. I want a man who holds me in his heart the way Jonathan held you. Did you know his relationship line didn't waver?"

"I didn't. No." She'd overheard Belinda's discovery of that in Jonathan's palm. And there was something about a new relationship, too, but she might have misread the line.

"Anyway, I'm lucky to know you both," Belinda said.

Esmeralda pushed away her worries and worked hard all day, approving four grants after interviews, recommending that four applicants attend a workshop to refine their requests and reading through a dozen proposals. She barely had time to let her intuition percolate with the shorter sessions, and she skimmed through the rubric, but what other choice did she have?

She reached home exhausted. The dogs greeted her cheerfully, and she buried her nose in their fur for long minutes. Tonight they would be leaving her.

She checked messages. A half-dozen friends and clients needed her help and no call from Lenore. She picked up the phone to start the callbacks, then put it down. She just couldn't be there for anyone else at the moment.

Her doorbell rang. Lindy Little early? She wasn't ready for that. Her heart in her throat, she went to the door, relieved to find it was Mitch.

Without a word she threw herself into his arms.

"What's wrong?" he asked immediately.

"It's been a long day," she said.

"What's really wrong?" he demanded.

"Someone's coming for Huffington. Pistol, too, probably."

"Really? That's a drag." He bent down to pet the dogs.

"They're going to a good home."

Mitch looked up at her, his eyes fierce and certain. "Don't give them up, Esmeralda."

"I promised. I'm just the foster person. That's the deal."

He stood and took her forearms. "When they get here, say you decided to adopt them."

She couldn't speak.

"You love them. You're crying."

She touched her cheek, surprised to find moisture there. "I'll miss them, that's all. Foster owners care, so of course they cry."

"Keep the dogs. You know you want to."

"Wanting isn't enough. If it were right, I would know it."

"You don't need a line on your palm to know when you love something and want it in your life. Can't you see that?"

That did it. He was supposed to comfort her, not dig at her. "Stop criticizing me, Mitch."

"I'm trying to help you."

"No you're not. You just want to be right."

"And you're afraid I am."

That stung. "I'm not like you, Mitch. I don't want to be like you."

The phone rang.

"Leave it. Give yourself some peace."

"That's not what brings peace for me. I don't see people as intrusions."

"Are you afraid to let yourself want something? Is that why you give yourself away to everyone else? You've got a big heart, Esmeralda. Plenty of room for two little dogs."

She wanted to cover her ears. Instead, she went for the phone, but then the doorbell rang and her blood ran cold. Lindy Little for sure.

"Could you get that?"

"You'll have to." Mitch stood by the door, arms folded, telling her with all his body language that she'd be making a mistake if she did.

"Honestly," she said, giving up on the phone to get the door. She shot him a scalding look before opening the door to a middle-aged brunette with a friendly face, a purse over her shoulder and a dog toy on one hand.

"Hi. I'm Lindy," she said and squatted to greet the dogs. "This is Huffington." She extended her empty hand for Huffington to sniff. Exactly the right approach. "And this guy's Pistol?"

"Yes," Esmie managed to say in a normal voice. She picked up only good vibes from the woman and sighed.

"Jill mentioned they're buddies. That I should take them both. Do you think that's right?"

"They'd be happier together," she choked out, hardly holding in the tears. She glanced at Mitch in mute misery.

He frowned and a muscle in his jaw ticked.

"I can try Pistol for the weekend to see how it works with two dogs. My place is kind of small. But you're so little, aren't you? Hardly any trouble, huh?" She rested her cheek against Pistol's mug. So sweet and loving. Perfect for them.

Esmeralda's whole body ached. She forced herself to get the cardboard box where she'd put Huffington's bed, kibble and the too-many toys she'd bought. She added Pistol's stuff and began explaining the things they liked, the special treats, how each preferred to be scratched, bathed and played with. Then she noticed that Lindy had a hand on the doorknob and the dogs leashed. She was nodding along, eyes glazed, while Esmeralda babbled.

"I should let you go," she said, sadness spearing her.

"I'll call if I have questions," Lindy said, backing out the door. The dogs paused, looking to Esmie, a question in their eyes, but when Mitch carried the box of dog stuff out the door—he'd watched the exchange in stony silence—they turned and trotted after him.

Esmeralda shut the door against the sight of her dogs leaving. She was still standing there when Mitch threw open the door and slammed it shut behind him. "There was no reason for that," he snapped.

"It's done. Stop talking about it. You're not helping me. Why don't you just leave?"

"I don't get you, Esmeralda."

"No, you don't. And I'm sick of hearing about it." The phone rang and she hurried to answer it. "Just go," she said, waving at him before she picked up the phone.

It was a telemarketer. When she hung up and turned,

she saw he'd done what she asked. *Be that way,* she thought. *Just leave. Walk away.* He was so self-righteous, judging her life, making her question things she took for granted.

How could they belong together? Far from being soul mates, they were uneasy allies, only united in bed. If they were meant to be together, she needed a better sign than she'd gotten so far.

What a bitter thought. Not like her at all. That was another thing—Mitch brought out her irritable side. Not good.

She sank onto the couch, fighting despair. Without the dogs, her house felt empty and too quiet. Wrong somehow. Why couldn't she have a pet anyway? Was she afraid to admit what she wanted like Mitch had said? No. It had to do with not getting attached, with treating hellos and goodbyes as just part of life.

After her mother died, she became tentative about the people she loved. She kept things light with friends and certainly with men.

She'd been that way with Jonathan, now that she thought about it. He'd been certain of them and she'd gone along, but she'd never really given herself to the relationship. She'd been sad when he left, but not devastated.

Because she'd never really been in love with him.

The realization hit her hard. Mitch made her question everything. Time faded while she let the implications trickle through her.

She came out of the trance to the sound of someone pounding on her door. Groggy on her feet, she went to the door.

It was Mitch with both dogs on their leashes, their box under his arm. The dogs lunged for her and Mitch released them, coming inside, too.

She sank to the floor, her skirt billowing out, trying to hug the dogs while they licked her and bumped her with wet noses. She was laughing and crying at once.

"Miss Lindy drives like a bat out of hell," Mitch said. "If she hadn't stopped for gas I would never have caught her."

She looked up at him. "What did you say to her?"

"I told her the dogs belong with you."

They yapped, bodies quivering, as if to affirm his words.

"Was she upset?"

"Not after I told her that when it rained, they preferred peeing on Oriental rugs to using the doggie door and weren't we in for some more storms? I threw in that they treated leather shoes like appetizers."

"You lied!"

"Had to." He shrugged.

"They do belong here," she said. "You were right. I need these guys." She thought about explaining about her mother's death and attachment issues, but looking into Mitch's face, she realized he already knew. "Maybe you do understand me," she said softly.

"Some of you," he said, dropping to the floor beside her, petting the dogs, though his eyes never left her face. "It'll take time to get the rest."

"Good things always do." The man had chased down a stranger to give her what she hadn't even admitted to herself she wanted. That was a sign, all right. And she knew something else for sure. She was falling in love with this man.

What to do about it was another matter. It was like those joke-fortune-telling Magic 8 Balls. *Reply hazy— try again later.*

13

"I HOPE YOU'RE NOT STARVING," Mitch warned Esmeralda, parking in front of his house, since Annika had taken over his spot in the garage. She'd made his brother so happy, he was delighted to hand it over to her.

Dale had insisted on cooking dinner for Esmie to thank her for introducing him to Annika.

"I'm sure whatever Dale cooks, I'll love," Esmeralda said, stubbornly optimistic, as always.

"Hold that thought, Little Miss Sunshine." He hardly minded her relentlessly positive spin on everything these days. Being with her during the week since he'd rescued her dogs seemed to have loosened bands around his chest he hadn't known were there. He'd always been watchful and careful, but he'd never realized what a strain it had been.

Something had happened when he brought back those dogs. He'd looked at her on the floor, her skirt a puddle of silk across her lap, the dogs snuffling around her, adoring her, as if she were the goddess of all things doggie and beautiful, and something inside him burst and spilled warmth everywhere.

She was his beautiful goddess, too—kooky psychic or not—and he never wanted to come up for air.

And he couldn't get enough of her body. In bed, she was a wicked angel, mischievous and creative, exploring every position, every sensation, all night long. But it was more than sex. She got into his head, moved things around, lit up his life, like that meteor shower spraying the sky.

You hopeless goofball. He was way out of his element, but he would ride it out, see what would happen. For once in his life, he was letting go.

Tonight he was silently celebrating because Craig had told him that no alarms had gone off from the information Mitch had passed to them the week before. He'd felt better about Belinda when she handed him updated financials without hesitation, as she'd promised. Maybe he'd just caught her off-guard that day. He'd dropped the report off with Craig without examining it. He was no accountant, after all.

It was a relief to forget his subterfuge at last. Now and then he had the uneasy sense he was doing some Esmeralda-style wishful thinking, but he was too happy to care.

Inside the house, nothing smelled bad. "So far, so good," he whispered to her. "No sign of fire extinguisher use."

"Stop it," she said, grinning at him. She would punch him, he knew, except her hands were busy with the giant fruit tart she'd insisted on making. Mitch had done everything but the crust, though, since she'd gotten tied up on the phone.

He hoped he was helping her with a little more balance, coaxing her into some call-screening with lips and tongue and fingertips. Her soft sighs were his greatest reward.

The woman needed help sorting out what she wanted. She hadn't known enough to keep a pet she loved. She needed to trust herself more, and he needed to help her.

And just maybe he needed her.

"Hey, there!" Dale said, heading for them. "This looks fantastic." He took the tart from her hands.

"The food smells great," Esmeralda said, taking a deep sniff of the room's air.

"Cornish game hens with crab apple-sage glaze, jalapeño jelly, pickled chiles and sweet-potato risotto. Come see." He waved them toward the kitchen, which was surprisingly neat. "Annika made me follow the recipes. Not very creative, but—"

"I bet it will be delicious," Mitch said, winking at Annika. Already she'd improved life around here. She could park in his spot forever, as far as he was concerned.

Soon they were seated at the table, enjoying the best meal Dale had ever prepared, but it was the company that made the night sparkle. Maybe Esmeralda had a point about his isolation. People weren't intrusions. When had he become such a grump, anyway?

"So, here's to Esmeralda," Dale said, lifting his glass. "For the grant, for Annika, for humanizing my brother."

"Hey—" Mitch started to object, then gave up. "Yeah," he said, turning to her. "Here's to that." He tapped his wineglass against hers and she smiled, her eyes shining at him.

"So, after dinner, will you read our palms?" Dale asked. "You can tell us if we're getting the grant and… other things?" He glanced at Annika, then back, going pink. Dale blushing? Annika was a wonder.

Esmeralda shot Mitch an uncertain look. "I don't think I'm up for that tonight." She bit her lip. She thought he didn't approve? "But you don't need me to read your palm to tell you your grant will be approved. You two did a great job."

They drank a toast to the grant, then Dale and Annika rose to clear the dishes.

Mitch leaned close, taking her hand. "If you want to read their palms, I'll be good." He'd come to an uneasy peace with her being psychic. When he thought of it at all, he considered it an unusual trait, like being double-jointed or having a photographic memory.

"I'm not really in the mood these days." She seemed troubled and uncertain in a way he'd never noticed before. Was it his influence?

"Hey, read my palm, if you want." He held it out.

She smiled. "You know I can't. When I care about someone, I can't give an accurate reading. I put too many hopes in it."

"And you have a lot of hopes for me?"

"I do," she said, but worry flickered in her eyes. It had to do with her ex-husband, he knew. Things would be better once she cleared the air with the guy, who'd be gone for still another week. Mitch had been glad of the uninterrupted time with Esmie, but it left them in a kind of airless suspension. Jon Boy was the wild card between them. Which made Mitch feel simultaneously more possessive of Esmeralda and more tentative about their future.

"You're tired," he said now, kissing the back of her hand. "We'll get to bed early tonight."

"We get to bed early every night, Mitch."

"But this time we'll actually sleep."

"If you say so." She smiled, then looked very tired. "I am kind of worn out. Getting ready for the board meeting is stressful. Nine more working days."

"You'll do great." Esmeralda had fine-tuned the business plan he'd drafted and had shown him the preliminary version of her presentation. She impressed him more each time they talked it over. She might have been ignorant about business concepts when she started, but in the three weeks since he'd known her, she'd earned the equivalent of an MBA. She was so smart, so savvy. He could almost forget that she read the auras of the grant applicants.

Almost.

"I'm worried that I rushed through the grants. The pressure made me cut corners on my process." She nibbled her lip, then sighed. "But never mind. I don't want to spoil tonight."

"You couldn't spoil it, Esmie." He linked fingers and kissed the back of her hand. "By the way, I'm sending Maggie to your workshop tomorrow night."

"Really?"

"Yes. She took her daughter to college over the weekend and called in sick today. She's never sick. Especially not on a Monday. I figured she was depressed. I know she doesn't want to become a paralegal, but she needs something. I'm hoping you'll help her figure out what it is."

"I'm happy to," she said. "I appreciate your faith in me." He'd quelled her doubts for the time being, so that was good.

After dinner, he tuned up his guitar and asked Dale

to play with him. It felt strange and right at the same time. Esmeralda was as enthralled as she'd been the night they met.

As he played, the old urge to make music rose in him. He felt no ambition, he just wanted the music for himself and those he loved. Looking into Esmeralda's eyes, he wanted to play and play. How had he let that slip away?

Maybe Esmeralda and Dale had been right and he'd given up something big when he put away his music.

Later, when he and Esmeralda lay naked together in her play pool just for the fun of it, laughing up at the night sky, he knew that if it all fell apart tomorrow, he was glad they'd been together. He would never be the same. And that was a good thing.

He wasn't a bit surprised when three stars flew across the sky. The Pleiades shower was long gone.

It had to be a sign.

"ESMERALDA, I NEED TO talk to you." Belinda stopped Esmie in the middle of a mad dash to the boardroom. It was an hour before the meeting and Esmeralda was jittery with tension. The copier had jammed making the packets, she'd accidentally deleted a presentation slide and the caterer had mislaid their order.

"Can it wait until after the meeting?" She tried for a patient tone.

"Not really." Belinda's face had red blotches and her eyes were shiny with anxiety. "You know I always did my best, Esmeralda, right?"

"Yes. You've been great." Belinda had been very helpful at the two workshops she'd attended and was drafting grants for three possible clients. "What is it?"

"I was looking over the books today, and there may be problems. You know Rico helped me? Well, there are changes—big ones—that I can't figure out and he won't return my calls."

"What do you mean, big changes?"

"Missing money. Or miscounted money. Or something. I don't know. Jonathan told me to talk to you, that you're so understanding."

"Okay…" And Jonathan had been giving Belinda advice? He'd returned from Brazil last night and was eager to talk with Esmeralda.

"What do you expect me to do about this now, Belinda? The board meeting's in an hour."

"I don't know. Nothing, I guess. The board materials only have a summary, so it should be okay for the meeting. We can talk after." She gnawed her lip.

"What else is it, Belinda?"

Belinda raised anguished eyes. "See, the thing is, remember that I was having trouble understanding Rico? Well, basically, Rico *did* the bookkeeping for me. I just copied it into the computer spreadsheet. Rico can be a little iffy about right and wrong. Not always, but sometimes."

She'd never met Rico, had trusted him because of Olivia and Belinda. She felt that prickle again. *This is bad. Look into this.* Belinda was still holding her breath, so there was more.

"And…?"

"And there's that one grant, the teddy bear one, from Rico's associates, remember? I have a bad feeling about it."

She'd rubber-stamped some of Belinda's recommendations, including that one. Hadn't even made an appointment with the applicant. More prickles flew along her nerves, accompanied by the trickle of ice water.

"We'll have to look into that later," she said. "For now, please set out these packets." She handed them to her and pushed Belinda's warning to the back of her awareness. What else could she do? She would face twenty board members in an hour, several of them skeptics. She had no room for doubts.

TWO HOURS LATER, ESMERALDA pointed to her final slide, which showed her investment capacity goal. "This is an ambitious goal, of course, but I hope you can see we are determined to get there. And we will. Little dreams for the little people can lead to a big success for us all. Thank you."

The applause was deafening. She almost laughed out loud. Her presentation had gone remarkably well, and here was the proof. Whatever problems Belinda had found in their finances, Esmie would handle later. For now, she basked in the glory of her accomplishment. Her mother must be so proud of her.

As the applause ended, Olivia rose to stand beside her at the podium. "Having you as our director, *cara,* has been a gift from heaven." She turned to the board seated in a circle around the table. "Did I not say she knew the human heart, Louis?"

"Yes, Livie, you always know best," he said with a sigh. There were genial chuckles all around.

"It's been an honor to work for you all," Esmeralda said to the group, then returned her gaze to Olivia. "And thank you, Olivia, for your faith in me."

She was so proud of herself. She only wished Mitch could have been here to share her triumph. He'd had client meetings this morning. She would call him as soon as she was free.

Applause started up again, signaling the end of the meeting. Through it, Esmeralda picked up on a commotion from up front. Belinda was yelling, her voice high, and there was another voice, low and urgent. Fast-moving footsteps approached.

"You can't go in there." Belinda's voice came from outside the door. Then a man in a short-sleeved shirt and tie came in, followed by two policemen. "Esmeralda McElroy?" he said.

When she nodded, he handed her several typed pages and introduced himself as a detective with the Phoenix police.

"These officers are here to execute a warrant to search the premises and remove all computers and documents pertaining to the Dream A Little Dream Foundation."

"What is this regarding?" Esmeralda asked, staring down at the paper, the words blurring before her eyes. There were seals and signatures and a long list of items.

"We're acting on behalf of the Arizona Attorney General's office," the detective said matter-of-factly, "related to alleged violations of federal and state laws pertaining to money laundering and drug smuggling."

"Drug smuggling?" Esmeralda felt like she might faint.

"This is outrageous," Olivia said to the detective.

Meanwhile, Esmie noticed that Olivia's brothers, Enzo and Louis, had disappeared.

"We'll gather what we need and be out of here," the

detective said to Esmeralda. "You'll hear from the A.G.'s office." He nodded good-bye and he and the policemen left the room.

All the remaining board members were talking loudly, or glued to cell phones or demanding an explanation. She had none, except to say, over and over, "This must be a mistake. It has to be a mistake."

"Not to worry, *cara*," Olivia said. "My attorney's on his way. My family has had its problems, but none of this concerns you or our foundation."

In a daze, Esmie went down the hall and watched the police carry her and Belinda's computers and files out the door. She tried to read the papers listing everything they could take, but it seemed like everything but the wallpaper.

Belinda kept wringing her hands and saying she was sorry. If there was something illegal going on, it might have to do with Rico's being *iffy with right and wrong*.

What should Esmie do now? She needed help, advice, someone to lean on. Mitch. Of course. And he was a lawyer. He would know what to do.

She called his office and was surprised when Maggie told her Mitch was already on his way over. Maybe to see how the board meeting had gone? Unless he'd picked up her distress telepathically. That made her smile a little, at least.

Olivia's attorney arrived and stayed just long enough to give Esmeralda a card and promise to be in touch before he hustled Olivia out the door.

Minutes after that, Mitch barreled in.

Esmeralda rose from the chair where she sat beside Belinda at the now-bare reception desk.

"I'm so sorry, Esmeralda," he said, as if he already knew what had happened.

"What do you mean?"

"I didn't know they were going for a warrant. My friend in the A.G.'s office only found out by a fluke. He's been on another case. Are you okay?" He tried to put his arms around her, but she backed away.

"You knew about this?" she asked, shocked. The truth of it fell through her body like a heavy weight. "Your friend in the A.G.'s office…? What are you telling me?"

"It wasn't supposed to come to anything. He told me there were no red flags. But the forensic accountant took a look and then the police searched the warehouse—"

"The warehouse? What warehouse?" A cold chill passed through her. There'd been some kind of investigation and Mitch had known. Had he been part of it?

She stared at him, shocked and hurt, not sure what question to ask first. Then she heard her name and saw Jonathan rushing in. "Are you all right?" he asked her, hugging her.

"I called him for you," Belinda said softly.

Esmeralda broke off the hug. "I'm okay. Just in shock."

"What happened?" Jonathan asked.

"I'm afraid it's Rico," Belinda cried. "He might have messed with the books, but we don't know anything for sure."

"Mitch does, however," Esmie said, the bitter taste in her mouth matching her words. "Why don't you tell us all what's going on?"

"We need to talk," Mitch said to her. "Privately."

"We'll work this out, Esmie," Jonathan said. "We'll sue the bastards. We'll take it to the media."

Mitch rolled his eyes.

But Esmeralda felt protective of Jonathan. He had no clue what had just happened, but he was ready to tilt the windmills, offer the grand gesture. Sweet, but also, she had to admit, not very useful.

It infuriated her that as angry as she was at Mitch, she depended on him for the facts. She knew she could count on him to be honest and direct and complete, to offer useful ideas, not wild-eyed promises.

Except the man had lied to her. He'd known about the investigation? Or even been part of it? That was even worse.

"Come on. I'll explain what I know." Mitch nodded toward the hall, wanting her office for privacy, no doubt.

"Do you want me to come with you?" Jonathan asked.

"I'm fine. You and Belinda go. Please. I'll call you both later when we've figured this all out."

She led Mitch to her office and they sat on the sofa where they'd once made love. Some desperate part of her wanted Mitch to explain it all away. She looked into his handsome face, the dark eyes that had sparkled with love and remembered they'd also held suspicion. From the very beginning, now that she thought about it. "You thought I was doing something illegal?"

"Not you. Never you. Before I came here about the grant, I asked my friend what he knew about the legitimacy of the foundation."

"You thought we were phony?"

"Come on. You were giving away money. It sounded too good to be true."

"To you, I suppose, it would." *Some people are crazy or crooks.* He'd told her that and asked about Olivia's money, wondered if her predecessor had been fired. He'd been suspicious from the beginning.

"It should have made you wonder, too. Did you know that Olivia is part of the Sylvestri crime family?"

"What?"

"Exactly. She and the two brothers on your board. Their older brother, Darien, is in prison right now for drug smuggling."

"You're kidding."

"No. I'm not. Craig recognized the name, did some checking and asked me to find out what I could." He had the decency to look chagrined.

"You were investigating me?"

"Not you. I knew you were innocent, but if it was an illegal operation, I wanted to get it stopped quickly, hopefully while protecting you at the same time."

"Oh, really? You were protecting me?"

"That was my intent. I got the files to Craig and as far as I knew nothing came of it."

"What files?"

"Tax records, the financial logs, all the grants. I got most of it from Belinda. I made some copies on my own."

"You made copies…. And you gave files to the Attorney General?"

"The idea was to find out what we could without alarming anyone engaged in wrongdoing."

"Like me, you mean?"

"Not you. Maybe Belinda. Olivia. Whoever. Anyway, Craig said nothing showed up at first, but there was a marked-up ledger that caught the forensic accountant's eye, plus one of the grants had been flagged. Teddy bears for a charity, something like that?"

The grant Rico's associates had wanted funded. That did fit with Belinda's worries. "What about it?"

"They searched a warehouse with hundreds of the bears, all stuffed with coke."

"No." Her body was heavy with dread and guilt. She should never have let the grants slide through on faith.

"It was similar to a scheme with a yarn shop owned by Darien Sylvestri's wife." He paused. "Weren't you suspicious, Esmie? When you interviewed the guy for the grant?"

"I didn't interview him. I had to rush some grants that Belinda prescreened. This was one of them. I should have stuck to my system. I'm responsible for this." The burden of her mistake was more than she could stand.

"What about Belinda?"

"She's not involved. It was her ex-boyfriend. He was showing her how to do the books. He worked for Olivia's brother. Belinda suspected something and tried to tell me."

"So Olivia and her brother could be behind this."

"Not Olivia. She couldn't be involved."

"You have too much faith in people."

"And you have none. Why didn't you talk to me? Ask me before sneaking around copying files. I would have helped you."

"You might have interfered."

"You think I would give aid to criminals?"

"If you thought they were innocent. I couldn't risk it. This was safer for you."

"Safer? I don't see how. Lies are never safe."

"I wasn't happy to be caught in the middle, but I

decided that if there were criminals involved I could keep you out of danger. And then it seemed like it was all clear."

"But it wasn't, was it?" She felt sick.

"I'm sorry. From what Craig says you won't be charged with anything. I'm not sure about Belinda."

"This is terrible. I can't believe it." She was a mess. Her feelings churned—shock, betrayal, disgust at herself, worry about her clients.

"Whatever I can do to help, I will, Esmie. Craig, too. He feels bad about how this went down. He'll keep the media away from you."

"Forget me. What about the people I gave grants to? The homeless program? The prostitute network? Cindy Sanders' scholarship? What about Dale and Annika?"

"They got caught in the net. They'll find other funding. Maybe loans."

"You know how unconventional some of the ideas were."

"I'll help however I can."

"You've done enough, don't you think?" she snapped at him. "You should go. I have to call everyone we said yes to and everyone attending our workshops to tell them that their dream is dead."

"Do you want me to do it? Would that help?"

"They're my calls to make," she said. "I should have been more careful. I shouldn't have rushed the grants. I shouldn't have ignored my instincts where Belinda was concerned."

"You did your best, Esmeralda. They'll understand."

"I don't see how. I don't understand." And she didn't understand how Mitch could have gone to bed with her after he'd turned over material to authorities that might shut down the foundation.

"I'll be in touch," he said and stood, looking down at her with regret and concern. "We'll work this out."

"I don't see how." She didn't.

She'd failed. She'd ignored her instincts, her psychic gifts, even her good sense. She'd failed Olivia, the foundation, her grantees and herself.

And she still loved Mitch. Which was no help at all. Her obsession with him had contributed to her failure, increased her doubts, made her second-guess herself.

She would not do what Zena had done. She would not tell herself that love would smooth the rough edges, make two people fit who had no business together.

She would make up for her mistakes as much as possible. And that meant ending things with Mitch.

14

THAT NIGHT, A MONSOON storm hit, matching the one in Esmeralda's life. The thunder sent the two dogs cowering under her bed. She was on her hands and knees, coaxing them out, when her doorbell rang.

Jonathan, she was sure. He'd taken Belinda home after the police visit and promised to come to show her support. She preferred to be alone, but they did need to talk. What she would say to him, she had no idea.

But it turned out to be Mitch at her door. He stood on the porch soaking wet, water dripping from his hair and sparkling on his cheeks. Behind him, thunder rumbled a distant threat from the darkened sky. Wordlessly, his eyes burning into her, Mitch waited for her to let him in.

She stepped back and he moved forward, bringing with him the creosote smell of wet desert and the warm humidity of the storm—smells she loved, but now made her weak with sadness.

The dogs forgot their storm fear and raced to greet Mitch, except once in sight of the two humans they began to pace and whine worriedly.

"Do you want something to drink? Some tea? A snack?"

He shook his head, sprinkling the floor with water.

"A towel then?" She tried to smile.

"I'm fine."

She led him to her sofa, choosing a distant chair for herself.

"How are you?" he asked.

"The attorney says we won't know the extent of the charges for a while."

"You should be okay though. Craig said that—"

"I'm not worried about me. I told you that before. But it seems that Olivia will be safe, too. Belinda could be complicit in the false books, but if she cooperates she should escape any charges. We don't know if the foundation will be able to continue. The publicity will be bad." Her voice shook and she couldn't go on.

"I'm so sorry."

"I know you are." She'd realize she was mostly angry at herself. Mitch had done what she would expect from him. And maybe it was good. At least he'd reminded her how insurmountable their differences were.

"If I'd used my gifts properly, stayed alert and sensitive, I could have picked up warnings, handled the problems sooner."

"Forget the mystical stuff. Trust your head and your heart. You're a smart lady. That's what counts."

"Don't dismiss my gifts," she snapped. "That's who I am."

"That's not all you are. Not by a long shot."

"You drag me down, Mitch. You make me doubt myself."

"I pull you into the real world. Why can't you trust what's real?"

"Why do you belittle what you don't understand?"

"Let's not argue."

"We have to. Don't you see. We're impossibly different."

"You're giving up on us? Just like that?"

"Just like that?" Her life was in ruins and he'd played a key role in her downfall. But why state the obvious? "We would only hurt each other."

"I never meant to hurt you."

"I know."

He held her gaze, his face sad, his mouth grim. "What will you do?" He sucked in a breath. "You're not going back to your ex, are you?"

"That's none of your business." She had no clue how she felt about Jonathan. Her instincts in her own life seemed utterly gone.

"That would be a bad idea." He said it low and sure. "You don't need a guy who'll smile and nod at whatever you say. You need someone who'll level with you. You don't need to be worshipped. You need to be grounded."

"I can tell you what I don't need—a man who belittles my beliefs and second-guesses everything I do."

"You're right." His shoulders sagged. "You can't stop believing in magic any more than I can start believing in it."

"At last we agree on something."

That wasn't quite fair. He'd said things that made sense to her now. She did tend to discount her head and heart. She did sometimes ignore her own needs. But what was the point in saying so now? It didn't change anything between them.

"I should go."

"You should." She felt the sharp pain she'd felt when her mother died. She missed her suddenly. Her mother had always helped her see the truth, even when it was hard.

"It'll be okay, Esmie," Mitch said. He lunged from the sofa to his knees and put his arms around her. "You'll get through this. I'll help however I can. I know the law. You can tell me I'm full of shit in every other area, but trust me on that. At least let me help you there."

She nodded against his wet hair. His damp shirt gave off the scent of laundry soap and his skin. Guiltily, she breathed him in, took comfort from his strong arms, the way he always made her feel safe.

They stayed that way for far too long. Neither of them wanted to let go.

The doorbell rang, ending the moment.

Mitch went with her to the door. Jonathan stood on her porch, shaking an umbrella free of water. His eyes lit when he saw her. "I'm a little late. I was—" He noticed Mitch. "Am I interrupting?"

"I'm leaving," Mitch said. He gave her a long look. "Take care of yourself, Esmeralda." He turned to Jonathan. "Don't hurt her or you'll answer to me."

She watched him stride off, all macho strut to anyone watching. Only she had seen the softness in his eyes, the loneliness, the longing—

"What's up with you two?" Jonathan asked gently.

"Nothing. It's over."

He searched her face. "You don't look like it's over."

"It was a mistake to get involved with him. We're too different. All we do is argue."

"I'm sorry you're in pain." Jonathan hugged her and she buried her face in his clean, dry shirt. Mitch's shirt had been soaked. He'd run to her, heedless of the weather. Jonathan had thought to bring an umbrella, which he set in the entryway to dry.

That was sensible of him. And careful. Who says Jonathan couldn't ground her? He was so much more grounded himself now.

Mitch was full of it.

She led Jonathan into the house. The dogs stayed at the door as if waiting for Mitch to return.

"Would you like some tea?" she asked.

"Love some." He followed her into the kitchen, while she prepared it. He seemed restless, though. She remembered that he'd had something on his mind to talk about, too, back before all this had happened.

Soon the tea sent fragrant wisps of healing chamomile into the air and they sat on the sofa where Mitch had been.

"There's water here." Jonathan scooted away from the spot where Mitch had sat.

She stared at it, feeling stupidly sentimental.

Jonathan grasped her fingers in a soft, friendly way. "I feel badly that I was gone when all this happened to you and Belinda. Maybe I could have prevented it."

"How could you have?" She was dismayed to see the I-will-fix-everything gleam in his eyes that used to drive her crazy. She always had to force him to face the facts of the problem.

"The point is to fix things now. And I can."

"How? It's up to the A.G. and the lawyers."

"I mean fix things with you. Finally, I can. Come to San Diego with me. You can work for me or not. You won't have to worry about money. I'll handle all that from now on."

"Jonathan, that's sweet of you, but—"

"You had the prediction, remember? And there's something else. Another reason I had to see you again. Even before I saw the newspaper story or Belinda sent me her copy."

"Belinda sent you a copy?"

"Oh. I forgot you didn't know. Yes, Belinda sent me the clipping with a Post-it note that said you were waiting for me."

"How did she even know who you were? I never mentioned—"

"She heard you talking to a friend. She did a Google search for my address. Anyway, I'd already clipped the article, but planned to wait until Travel Experiences was more established. But Belinda called and left me a message to come *now*."

"Belinda *called* you…?" She couldn't believe it.

"When you started seeing Mitch. She wanted to help. But the point is, my real reason to see you—"

"What was it?" Her head was spinning with this new information.

"When I was starting my business, I requested a credit report and it included you. I checked into it and the thing is…" He paused, swallowed hard, then looked into her eyes. "We're still married, Esmie."

"What?" She blinked, not sure she'd heard him correctly over the rumble of thunder outside.

"I filed the divorce papers, I swear. I stamped the envelope—everything—but I was so upset, who knows what I did."

"You're kidding." The realization rioted through her and the floor seemed to shiver under her feet. She was still married. Had been for the six years she'd assumed she was single. Was this why no one had clicked? Why she'd felt suspended in air? Why she'd expected Jonathan to return?

"I thought of telling you right off, but that felt like pressure. It seemed better to see how we felt about each other without the marriage hanging in the air, you know?"

"I guess." She could see that. She felt fuzzy, like a TV off its station. The dogs whined and circled again.

"Now, considering the trouble you're in, it makes sense that we're still married." He sounded sad when he said it. "All you have to do is take my name again and Esmeralda Walters can start new in San Diego. No one will ever have to know."

What he was saying made sense, of course. But there was something wrong with his saying it. He seemed full of grief and too much sadness. A spiritual awareness swirled through her, making her dizzy.

"I know it's a shock," he continued. "It won't be easy. But love is never easy. The way is rocky, the path winding and steep."

She got a flash of him running into the foundation office earlier, the look he'd given Belinda. Wait a minute…

Jonathan was babbling on, covering his pain with words. "So we begin anew, just like the prediction, right? That's it, don't you think? What it means?" His voice cracked. "I wanted to pay you back and now I can. I can do the right thing."

"The right thing…?" You didn't marry someone—or *stay* married to them—because it was the right thing. You did it out of love and commitment and a sense of forever.

And she and Jonathan did not have that. But there

was more going on. The truth was coming—roiling, spinning, tingling through her, filling her with its power. Belinda. And Jonathan.

Of course.

"You and Belinda…are you…together?"

Jonathan's face folded. "No. We're not. I mean, we want to be, but it's not right. She reminded me of you, I guess, and we worked together over the grant and talked and talked. We've been each other's coaches. But that's over." He sat up taller. "We both agree this is right. It was Belinda's idea, really. We both owe you so much." He swallowed hard. "All you and I need is more time."

Esmeralda smiled, sure of what she would say, calm in her knowledge of what to do. "We've had plenty of time, Jonathan."

What?"

"Our marriage is over. We're friends now. You're in love with Belinda. You belong with her."

"But I want to help you," he said, his face flaming red.

"You have. You've helped me see things clearly for the first time in a long time." Her instincts had kicked in at last. She couldn't be with Jonathan. That was clear. Far from beginning anew with a man from her past, she'd ended it with both of them. She'd had it with predictions.

What happened from here on in, she'd figure out on her own.

THE NEXT EVENING, Esmeralda was due to meet Sugar at Moons to see Autumn's farewell burlesque performance. She'd been looking forward to seeing her best friends until everything had fallen apart in her life. Now she didn't know how she could face them.

They wanted to celebrate the new love in both their lives and the changes she'd predicted, but Esmie had more doubts than ever about her gifts.

The poster for Let Us Entertain You inside the entrance to Moons was big and beautiful. The revue was very popular, but Autumn was giving it all up to be with the man she loved. On their thirty-fifth birthday, Esmeralda had predicted changes for Autumn in "hearth, head and heart…and heart would lead." Knowing Autumn to be a stubbornly unromantic realist, Esmie had a hard time believing she'd been right.

"Over here!"

She looked up to see Sugar waving to her from a front table, so she headed over for a big, slow hug. Unheard of for Sugar, famous for fast, bruising squeezes. The slow embrace soothed Esmeralda's ruffled soul.

"God, it's good to see you!" Sugar said in her husky alto.

"Love seems to agree with you." Esmeralda grinned.

"You're not saying I told you so, now, are you?" Sugar drawled. "That wouldn't be polite at all."

"I'm just saying you look happy. And that was the longest hug I've ever gotten from you."

"Isn't it weird? Love is something else. And you wouldn't believe Autumn. She's insanely dreamy."

"Autumn? Dreamy? I can't imagine." Autumn was the most down-to-earth, straight shooter Esmeralda knew.

"Sure you can. You predicted it. I can't wait for April to roll around. You gotta read my palms or my tea leaves or, hell, my underarm stains. I have to know what's next."

"I'm not up for readings tonight."

"What?" Sugar's therapist eyes honed in. "Hey… If I could read auras, I'd say yours was a monsoon cloud."

"Good eye." She tried to smile.

Before Sugar could probe, Autumn bounded out wearing a glittery, feathered bikini and a plumed head-dress and threw her arms around Esmeralda. Sugar was staying in Autumn's townhouse, so the two had already caught up. "Thanks for coming, Esmie."

"You look gorgeous."

Autumn tugged at her bra top. "God, this thing itches. I'll be glad to be done with it."

"So no regrets about quitting?"

"None whatsoever. I've got school—U of A—and I'm job-sharing with the town accountant. It's Plan B, but I've never been so happy." She smiled, then stared at Esmie. "Hey… What's up? Where's our Sister Serenity?"

"On sabbatical." She tried another weak smile.

"That's not you," Autumn said. "You always say it's darkest before the smog…every cloud has a silver thong…what doesn't kill us gets us arrested, all those great sayings." Autumn dropped into a chair, careful of her tail feathers, and motioned Esmie down. "Tell us everything. Leave out no juicy detail."

Esmeralda explained what had happened, her voice shaky.

"Oh, hon. Stone bummer," Autumn said when she'd finished, grabbing one hand.

Sugar grabbed the other. "We have to talk to that boy."

"It wasn't him. I was the one who broke it off."

"But you love him," Sugar said. "It's obvious. Plus you got three predictions. You're supposed to begin anew, yada, yada."

"I've figured that out." Though she would be happier when Lenore confirmed her theory. Lenore had left her a fuzzy voice mail from somewhere in India saying they'd talk when she returned to Arizona.

"Yeah?" The two friends looked at each other, then her.

"Jonathan and I began anew by restoring our friendship and finally ending our marriage. We have our lives back now. We're whole."

"But Mitch was from the past, too," Autumn said.

"Not really. Doctor X was the man I met. Mitch is different." *Not quite* and she'd seen more of Doctor X as Mitch lowered his defenses in her arms.

The two friends looked at each other.

"In denial?" Autumn asked.

"Absolutely," Sugar declared. She turned to Esmeralda. "You're in denial and you're so shaky. What's that about?"

She swallowed. "I feel lost, like my skills are gone."

"Like when your mom died? That kind of lost?" Sugar's training as a therapist was showing now.

She nodded.

"How did you overcome it then?"

"My mother came to me and told me not to give up."

"So what would she tell you now? Close your eyes and imagine it."

Esmie closed her eyes, took a slow breath and focused in. She felt a wave of love, as if she were wrapped in her mother's arms. She opened her eyes. "She would tell me to use my gifts, to be all that I am."

"Problem solved," Autumn said, dusting her palms together.

"It's not that easy," Sugar said. "It takes time to come

to grips with our doubts. You and I thought we didn't have the happily-ever-after gene, remember?"

"That's true. Hmm." Autumn tapped her chin with a nail. "Maybe you just need practice. You got your cards?"

Esmie hugged her satchel to her chest. "I'm not in a good space right now. I haven't felt like doing readings in a while."

"So what are you scared of about Mitch?" Autumn demanded, looking serious, despite the bikini and plumes.

"We're different. He doesn't respect my gift. He criticizes me. He makes me question myself."

"That's not always bad," Autumn said. "Mike and I are worlds apart, but we teach each other things. I teach him to lighten up and he holds up a mirror to my defensiveness. Hey…that's pretty shrinky of me, huh?" She elbowed Sugar.

"Oh, yeah. That and five bucks will get you a latte at Starbucks." Sugar turned to Esmie. "Where *did* you connect?"

"Sex. We're great in bed." She blushed.

"So start there."

"Spoken like a sex therapist," Autumn said. "Everything's not always about sex." She sighed. "But it can be damn close."

"Sex reflects the relationship," Sugar said. "It sounds like Mitch is the first man you've been truly intimate with."

Esmie sucked in a breath. "That might be true." She'd considered sex fun and friendly, but she'd always held herself back to some degree. Until Mitch.

"I was like that. I just floated along, enjoying the physical act, but not really being there. When you truly *bond,* when it's two-become-one in bed, that's true intimacy."

"You're smarter than you look," Autumn said.

"I'll take that as a compliment." Sugar turned to Esmie. "Think about it. Take some time."

"Thanks, Sugar. Thanks both of you. For being here." She squeezed both their hands.

"I've got an idea for something new you can read," Autumn said. She leaned over the table and shimmied her nearly bare breasts, sending a streak of glitter that looked remarkably like a meteor tail, across the table. "There. What does that mean?"

Esmie laughed, grateful for her friends. A cool breeze passed through her, as soothing as her mother's palm on her flu-hot forehead.

She felt it then. She would figure this out. It had to do with intimacy and lessons to learn and her mother's love. And a streak of glitter that reminded her of falling stars.

15

FOR THE NEXT WEEK, ESMERALDA turned inward. She referred out her palm clients and did only enough nails to pay her bills. It was difficult to disappoint everyone, but she needed the time, the quiet, the space.

Her phone rang off the hook, but she forced herself to let the machine take messages and returned only emergency calls. She needed time for herself, for once. Mitch had had a point about her sacrificing too much of herself to others.

Mitch. How she missed his comforting solidity. She ached for the security of his embrace. Mostly, she played with her dogs, who offered their scruffy love any time she opened her arms.

She was struggling to accept her failure with the foundation. She felt like she'd let everyone down, especially her mother. Her palm readings and advice seemed so puny after all she'd been doing through Dream A Little Dream. And she couldn't even manage a reading these days.

Sugar declared her depressed and called every day from San Diego with a life-affirming assignment. *Get a haircut, write in your journal, make a nice meal, get a massage.*

Autumn harangued her more bluntly from Copper

Corners. *Call the man. Get a grip. Stop moping. Read the damn cards.*

Esmeralda took it all in, listening to them and herself. She needed time. She was waiting for something to click in, fall into place, come clear. In short, a sign.

The news on the foundation was relatively good. Only Belinda's ex-boyfriend Rico would be charged with anything—fraud over the false books and drug-smuggling because of the coke-stuffed teddy bears. Other criminals had been arrested, but they had no affiliation with the foundation.

Olivia did not want to press charges against her brothers for the skimming they'd been doing through Rico. Whether or not the foundation would reopen would be up in the air for months.

Tuesday night arrived and Esmeralda's heart burned just as it had last week. It was workshop night. She could still hear the heartbreak in the voices of the grantees when she'd called to break the news to them. They'd tried to be brave, but there was no hiding the fact that their dreams had been dashed and it was her fault.

Go to a movie on Tuesday nights. That was Sugar's advice, but she didn't have the energy to leave the house. She settled in to play catch with the dogs, watching the clock slowly tick away the minutes of her failure.

The doorbell rang. Just Jimbo after her car, she hoped. She wasn't up for company. Except, through the keyhole, she saw a crowd, led by Belinda. She opened the door to her workshop people, arms loaded with wrapped dishes, six-packs of soda and beer, poster board and easels.

Huh?

"We're here for the Dream Workshop," Belinda declared.

"But this time we're brainstorming for you," Annika said, Dale at her side.

"My brother is an ass," he murmured to Esmie.

"But...I don't— You shouldn't—"

"Back away from the door, soldier," Maggie, Mitch's secretary, said. She'd uncovered her dream of doing stand-up comedy at the very last workshop Esmie had held. "We're helping you if we have to handcuff you to the chair."

While everyone unloaded their items and set up, Belinda led her down the hall for a private moment.

"This isn't necessary," Esmie said. "I appreciate the thought, but I'm fine."

"We need to help you," Belinda said. "It's a gift for us to give to you after all you've given to us. Oh, that sounds stupid, but you know what I mean." She grinned.

Love had done wonderful things for Belinda. She seemed more confident and stable. She would move to San Diego soon, where she'd work for Jonathan. Esmie wished them both well and had told them so over a dinner Belinda had cooked.

"I can never repay you," Belinda said, tears in her eyes.

"You made the changes yourself, Belinda. I wish I'd been more of a mentor to you."

"I tried so hard to be like you I couldn't see my own strengths. That's where Jonathan helped me. I'm a darn good writer, you know. The grant I wrote is good enough we're using it to apply for a business loan."

"That's good news," Esmie said.

"Now, how about you and Mitch?"

"We didn't work out."

"You have to. I mean I thought he was an ass at first, because of Jonathan, and he was just…well, an ass. But I saw your aura when you were with him. Plus it was predicted."

"We'll have to see," she said, wanting the conversation over.

"Do you want a reading? I'm getting better every day. You know I read in Jonathan's palm that he wasn't divorced. And I read about him and me, too. So, you taught me well."

"I'm not ready for a reading." She wasn't even sure she wanted Lenore to give her one when she returned from India.

"I won't rest until you're as happy as I am," Belinda said. "So you can expect to hear from me on a regular basis."

Oh, dear. "I appreciate that, Belinda. And the meeting is a nice gesture, but it's not necessary."

She headed into the living room to send everyone home with thanks. Her failure was a stab of cold steel in her heart. She couldn't imagine what her next career step would be or when she'd be ready to take it.

Everyone was so busy talking she couldn't have interrupted if she'd banged a gong. So she listened.

Duke was going forward with his plan to coach his employees. "I'm doing it on my own dime, goddammit. This can't die."

Dale had a line on a grant from the Music Foundation and Annika had set up a meeting with the state education department.

Valerie had gotten investors to get her custom lingerie company off the ground.

Cindy Sanders was doing a work-study with the A.S.U. preschool program.

One after another, her clients reported their next steps, their Plan B's, showing such indomitable determination she felt tears spring to her eyes. They'd been through doubts and work and worry and failure and they were keeping on.

How could she do less?

She made her way to the chair they'd saved for her facing a newsprint tablet with Esmie's Dreams written above the blank page, snowy white and inviting.

"Shall we get started?" she said. She could almost feel her mother's hand on her shoulder.

Before long, they'd generated a list of non-profits where Esmie might apply for a job, but more importantly, brainstormed a to-do list for creating her own foundation. It was an incredible, impossible idea, but it felt absolutely right.

"Thank you all," she said at the end. "This means so much."

"Build a plan, step by step to the stars, never give up," Annika said. "Repeat after us."

She did the affirmation, feeling shy and hopeful and stronger by the minute.

After they'd all gone, the echoes of their energy and support lingered, whisking over her like happy shadows of racing clouds or the streaks of warm water in a sunlit pool.

Sitting there, she'd realized something that had been slowly coming to her these weeks. There was a time to lean on readings and a time to depend on herself, her thoughts, her feelings, her own intuition.

Trust your head and your heart, Mitch had said.

She needed to balance psychic messages with her own good sense. He was right about that.

When the phone rang, she wasn't surprised it was Lenore. The moment she'd stopped craving an answer, it came to her.

Lenore asked her to come read palms with her at the Strawberry Festival in Strawberry, Arizona. It was a three-hour, winding drive from Phoenix, but Esmeralda couldn't say yes fast enough.

MITCH TOSSED OFF THE COVERS. Again. It was damned hard to sleep in this house without Dale making the usual noise, sending the comforting smell of bad cooking into the air. Dale had moved in with Annika, who'd scored a house-sitting gig across town, and now Mitch was one lonely, miserable guy.

He caught a whiff of strawberries from the ice-cream bowl beside his bed. Dale, who came over to play guitar with him every couple days, had brought a carton of ice cream tonight.

Tomorrow night, Dale and Annika were going to Esmeralda's with a bunch of workshop people to give her a dream session. Mitch was glad. He'd love to be there, but he couldn't bear seeing her again. He'd lost her job for her, after all.

He'd been playing a lot of music lately. Writing even. Partly because Dale had taken the sound system when he moved, so until he could buy his own stereo—tag, he was it. It also soothed him, taking him back to the joy of just playing, without wanting more. Just melody and rhythm, lyrics and chords.

Esmie had been right that he'd given up part of himself when he gave up music.

God, he missed her. Dale kept nagging him to talk to her. But what the hell would he say? Maybe he could see her differently, accept her crazy beliefs? It was possible. He sure saw Dale differently—as an adult in his own right, making his own reasonable choices, not someone whose life needed organizing into a shape Mitch recognized. Damn, he'd been arrogant. Dale was working it out just fine on his own.

He checked the clock. One in the morning. He tossed and thought and pounded his pillow and thought some more. Two-thirty. Damn.

He must have drifted off for a while because when he felt a hand on his shoulder he jumped, opening his eyes. There was the overwhelming scent of fresh strawberries and he saw a woman smiling down at him from the end of his bed. She looked like Esmeralda, except older, with wavy blond hair, a loose dress and the same sweet smile.

"I so wanted to meet you," she said.

"You're Esmie's mother," he said, knowing it instantly. She seemed damn real for a dream.

"She told me about you that night, you know. You're every bit as handsome as she said."

"Thanks," he said, feeling foolish.

"Will you give her a message from her grandmother?"

"Sure." This better be a dream or he was going crazy.

"Remind her of the spinach and the strawberries."

"The spinach and the…?"

"She'll understand." And she was gone.

In the morning, when he woke, he smelled strawberries again and his heart began to pound. Maybe she was back. Then he noticed the empty ice-cream bowl.

It was a dream, you idiot.

He missed Esmie so much he was making up visions of her dead mother. *Spinach and strawberries?* Huh? He got the paper and made his way to the kitchen for a bowl of his brother's leftover Cap'n Crunch.

As he ate, milk dropped onto the entertainment section. Brushing it off, he noticed the calendar listings. A festival in Strawberry. That was where? North, near Payson, he thought. This weekend. *Hmm.* Scanning the activities, the words *Fortune-telling By Lenore* jumped out at him, glowing, 3-D, before his eyes. Lenore… strawberries…Esmeralda's mother and her cryptic request. It all added up in a bizarre way he wasn't about to think through.

Because he had to do something about Esmeralda. He had to get her in his life. When he was with her, he felt open and alive, the way he had felt that night under the stars seventeen years ago.

Maybe he'd let in a little of her otherworldly stuff. Where was the harm? Life didn't have to be either-or. It was a balancing act, and Esmeralda, with her dancing eyes, wicked wit, and sun-bright hope, could show him that.

Maybe there was more to the world than he'd seen. He was willing to give it a try for Esmeralda's sake. Besides, he had to give Esmeralda her mother's message, didn't he?

16

CLIMBING INTO THE COOL PINE country, Esmeralda was more and more pleased about Lenore's invitation. Armed with new confidence in her abilities, she was ready to read palms again. The time she'd spent alone in the past two weeks—meditating, thinking, reading and resting—had given her new resolve to stay balanced in her life, to depend on herself as well as the psychic messages she picked up from the universe.

She still ached for Mitch and needed to talk with him. *Soon enough,* the message came to her and she held it close to her heart. Not second-guessing, not wrestling it into shape, letting it be. She would trust herself. And Mitch.

She passed fields of daisies all the way, which reminded her of her mother, whose presence had stayed with her since her very own Dream Workshop, where she'd decided what she wanted to do. She would be all right.

The festival grounds were busy, but not swamped when she arrived, inhaling the cool pine air, happy to be here. Wild anticipation shivered through her. She was glad to read hands again, but that didn't explain the quivering of her nerves or her difficulty breathing. Heat and light seemed to pour from her. Anyone who read her aura might think she was an astral projection, not really there.

She passed craft booths, then the food booths where the smell of strawberries filled the air. There were crates of fresh strawberries, strawberry jams and pies and sachets and tarts and candies.

Strawberries were special to her, so this was a fitting re-entry into palm reading. Lenore had said they were raising money for a children's fund. Squinting, she spotted Lenore's sign toward the far end of the park. She had a cheerful tent, and when Esmeralda looked inside, she couldn't believe that Mitch sat in a chair beside Lenore.

"Esmie," he said, rising.

"What are you doing here?" Her heart filled her throat and she knew this was what she'd sensed.

"I was hoping you'd read my palm." He held it out, face up, fingers spread. She remembered how he'd hidden it from her that first day when she'd asked to read it.

"Are you kidding me?" She turned to the smiling Lenore.

"He called right after I invited you," Lenore said.

"I figured that was a sign," he said, uneasy with the words, but saying them for her, she could tell. "A sign that Doctor X needed to show up again. I kind of buried that guy and I guess I need him. Just like I need Lady E."

"I'm so glad to hear that." Delight and hope lifted her off her feet until she felt as though she bobbed above the ground.

"He called to ask me to do a reading for him and you," Lenore added gently, as if prompting him to explain.

"I know that's what you would want," he said. She was touched by the generosity of his gesture, the humility of it.

"I think we both know all we need to know," she said.

Mitch shot Lenore a glance of thanks. Lenore smiled in silent blessing. "Come on," he said and took Esmie's hand in his sure, possessive way. She'd never realized she needed that kind of assurance. Not *needed* it. Valued it. She valued the strength and support Mitch offered her.

Jonathan's support was full of words and high wishes. But Mitch's was solid and grounded and it included the truth even when it might hurt. He would be there for the fallout, to make things right, to offer comfort and a hand at her back.

He led her to a bench under a tall pine in a quiet spot. The hum of the festival and the music-box song of a merry-go-round brought back the night they'd met. The air had an edge of coolness and smelled of strawberries and pine trees and rich soil.

They sat close together, knees touching, still holding hands. Mitch smiled. "I thought that since we first met at a fair with Lenore, this was the right place to start again."

"That's so sentimental." Her heart had blocked her throat completely.

"Not like me at all, huh?" He grinned.

"Not a bit." They both laughed and she realized they would do a lot of that. No matter their differences, they'd always been able to tease each other.

"It's your fault," he said. "I almost stopped on the way for an armload of daisies, but I know you like them alive, not dying in a vase."

It was true. She was startled to realize that was what had bothered her about the flowers Jonathan had brought her. Mitch did know her, in some ways better than she knew herself.

Then his face filled with emotion. "I missed you,

Esmie. I had a great life, but now it feels empty without you in it."

"I know what you mean. I've actually emptied my life out a little. I've done a lot of call-screening lately. I needed that. You were right."

He didn't say, *I told you so.* He just smiled, happy for her. "There's more to the world than meets the eye," he said slowly. "I can accept that."

"You can?"

"I'm beginning to." He studied her. "Does the phrase *the spinach and the strawberries* mean anything to you?"

"The spinach and the…? Yes." It was something her grandmother had said to her when she was a little girl. "Where did you hear that?"

"You're the only person I know who won't think I'm crazy when I tell you this, but your mother came to me—maybe in a dream, who knows?—and said your grandmother wanted to remind you about the spinach and the strawberries."

"That's amazing," she said, tears springing to her eyes. "What does it mean?"

"My grandmother babysat me and she was a strict health-food person, making me drink nasty seaweed and lemon grass goop. I would throw fits until she finally settled on spinach, which I could stand, but barely. If I ate my spinach, she'd give me the fruits I craved, as long as they had vitamin C. Luckily strawberries had plenty of it and I loved them.

"One day, when I'd barely nibbled the spinach, she set the strawberries in front of me and said, *Esmeralda McElroy, get that scowl off your face because the man you need will be spinach to your strawberries.*

"Huh. Interesting," Mitch said, a slow smile crossing his face. "I think I like your grandmother. And I've always liked vegetables."

"That figures," she said, happy to realize she had lessons to learn from this man and comforted that her mother and grandmother wanted to reassure her. She would not be Zena, hiding her gift from the man she loved.

"She looked just like you only older," Mitch said softly.

"Did she say anything else?" Her voice shook.

"That you talked about me the night we met."

"I did." The tears slid down her cheeks. "I told her you were an amazing musician and that I felt right around you."

"I don't know what I believe any more, Esmie, but if psychic stuff is important to you, then it's important to me. You can read my palm, my tea leaves, hell, the gray hairs on my head. Whatever it takes to keep you. We belong together."

"I need you to ground me, Mitch."

"And I need you to keep music in my life. I thought I wanted a career change, but what I needed was you."

"I think we can learn from each other…about fate and dreams and love and hope."

"And spinach?" he said, grinning.

"And spinach." She grinned back.

"So, your prediction came true, anyway. I'm the man from your past after all."

"I'd rather think of you as the man in my future." She moved into his lap for a hug that felt like coming home and a long and lovely kiss that tasted of heaven.

She pulled back and smiled softly. "I think somewhere a star crossed the sky."

"Does that mean I'm getting laid tonight?"

"There's a cute little place up the highway."

"I can't wait. I want to see your eyes glow for me again."

And she knew as long as she had him to help her balance wishes, dreams and reality, her eyes would shine forever.

Epilogue

"HERE'S TO TURNING THIRTY-SIX," Esmeralda said, raising her prickly pear margarita in salute to Sugar and Autumn. It was April, eight months since she and Mitch had found each other. Again and for good.

"Here, here," Sugar said. "I can't believe all that's happened in the past year." Sugar was pregnant and glowing. She and her partner, Gage, were getting married at their sex resort next month—reunion week, which was significant in their relationship. Autumn and Esmie would be bridesmaids.

"Here comes the big, fat bride, but oh, well." Sugar grinned. Gage had helped Sugar give up her headlong rush past the roses, so that now she stopped to inhale each passing petal.

"We're, like, totally different women," Autumn added. She would finish her degree and was running for mayor of the small town where she lived with Mike, the current mayor. He was impatient to tie the knot, but Autumn insisted they wait until after the election. "I refuse to run as Mayor Mike's wife. I want people to vote for former stripper Autumn Beshkin. Period."

So Autumn.

Esmeralda would never say "I told you so" to her

friends, but her predictions had been right on in both cases. *Love will transform your lives.* Of course she hadn't put it in those words exactly or her friends would have tossed their margaritas at her. The skill of a psychic lay as much in knowing what to withhold as what to reveal.

Besides, predictions were tricky things, she'd learned all on her own. With a little help from her mother and grandmother and Mr. Spinach, as Mitch now called himself whenever he questioned one of her impulses.

Mitch was having a drink at the bar with Gage and Mike before he had to start his set. He and Dale were trying out a drummer for their new band. He was having so much fun with his music, he seemed more like Doctor X every day.

Mitch seemed to sense her attention and raised his drink and winked at her. It was a prickly pear margarita. Mitch was secure enough in his manhood to drink an umbrella drink in her honor.

"You're whipped, boy."

Mitch set down the goofy drink and shrugged at Gage. "Takes one to know one."

"Oh, yeah," Gage said, looking over at his pregnant fiancée.

"So now the deal is that Esmeralda does a birthday reading for Sugar and Autumn?" he asked Gage.

"That's what I hear."

"Yeah. It was her tea leaves that got us into this mess," Mike said in mock gloom. "I hope to hell she doesn't come up with anything like Autumn opening a strip club in Copper Corners."

"Or triplets for us," Gage added.

All three men groaned.

"How do you deal with that mystical business anyway?" Gage asked Mitch.

"I don't really get it, but Esmie knows what she's doing. I trust her. She's amazing."

"I think they're all pretty great," Gage said, lifting his beer in the direction of the three women, now laughing together.

"Here's to three amazing women," Mitch said. He could hear Esmeralda's laugh above the others, light and sweet and high.

He was startled to notice a yellow glow near her head.

No. Not possible. Now he was seeing auras?

"What's wrong?" Mike asked. "You just see a ghost?"

"Worse, I think." Calling over the bartender, he ordered a shot of tequila. He was either becoming psychic or going crazy. Being in love with Esmeralda, with all the joy and surprise that entailed, he didn't care which.

* * * * *

Look for the next book from Dawn Atkins
as she hits the Malibu beach
for some sexy fun in the sun!
Coming in September 2007 from Harlequin Blaze.

Set in darkness beyond the ordinary world.
Passionate tales of life and death.
With characters' lives ruled by laws the everyday
world can't begin to imagine.

n●cturne

It's time to discover the Raintree trilogy....

New York Times *bestselling author*
LINDA HOWARD
brings you the dramatic first book
RAINTREE: INFERNO

The Ansara Wizards are rising and the Raintree clan
must rejoin the battle against their foes, testing their
powers, relationships and forcing upon them lives
they never could have imagined before....

Turn the page for a sneak preview
of the captivating first book
in the Raintree trilogy,
RAINTREE: INFERNO
by LINDA HOWARD
On sale April 25.

Dante Raintree stood with his arms crossed as he watched the woman on the monitor. The image was in black and white to better show details; color distracted the brain. He focused on her hands, watching every move she made, but what struck him most was how uncommonly *still* she was. She didn't fidget or play with her chips, or look around at the other players. She peeked once at her down card, then didn't touch it again, signaling for another hit by tapping a fingernail on the table. Just because she didn't seem to be paying attention to the other players, though, didn't mean she was as unaware as she seemed.

"What's her name?" Dante asked.

"Lorna Clay," replied his chief of security, Al Rayburn.

"At first I thought she was counting, but she doesn't pay enough attention."

"She's paying attention, all right," Dante murmured. "You just don't see her doing it." A card counter had to remember every card played. Supposedly counting cards was impossible with the number of decks used by the casinos, but there were those rare individuals who could calculate the odds even with multiple decks.

"I thought that, too," said Al. "But look at this piece of

tape coming up. Someone she knows comes up to her and speaks, she looks around and starts chatting, completely misses the play of the people to her left—and doesn't look around even when the deal comes back to her, just taps that finger. And damn if she didn't win. Again."

Dante watched the tape, rewound it, watched it again. Then he watched it a third time. There had to be something he was missing, because he couldn't pick out a single giveaway.

"If she's cheating," Al said with something like respect, "she's the best I've ever seen."

"What does your gut say?"

Al scratched the side of his jaw, considering. Finally, he said, "If she isn't cheating, she's the luckiest person walking. She wins. Week in, week out, she wins. Never a huge amount, but I ran the numbers and she's into us for about five grand a week. Hell, boss, on her way out of the casino she'll stop by a slot machine, feed a dollar in and walk away with at least fifty. It's never the same machine, either. I've had her watched, I've had her followed, I've even looked for the same faces in the casino every time she's in here, and I can't find a common denominator."

"Is she here now?"

"She came in about half an hour ago. She's playing blackjack, as usual."

"Bring her to my office," Dante said, making a swift decision. "Don't make a scene."

"Got it," said Al, turning on his heel and leaving the security center.

Dante left, too, going up to his office. His face was calm. Normally he would leave it to Al to deal with a cheater, but he was curious. How was she doing it? There were a lot of bad cheaters, a few good ones, and every so often one would come along who was the stuff of which legends were made: the cheater who didn't get caught, even when people were alert and the camera was on him—or, in this case, her.

It was possible to simply be lucky, as most people understood luck. Chance could turn a habitual loser into a big-time winner. Casinos, in fact, thrived on that hope. But luck itself wasn't habitual, and he knew that what passed for luck was often something else: cheating. And there was the other kind of luck, the kind he himself possessed, but it depended not on chance but on who and what he was. He knew it was an innate power and not Dame Fortune's erratic smile. Since power like his was rare, the odds made it likely the woman he'd been watching was merely a very clever cheat.

Her skill could provide her with a very good living, he thought, doing some swift calculations in his head. Five grand a week equaled $260,000 a year, and that was just from his casino. She probably hit them all, careful to keep the numbers relatively low so she stayed under the radar.

He wondered how long she'd been taking him, how long she'd been winning a little here, a little there, before Al noticed.

The curtains were open on the wall-to-wall window in his office, giving the impression, when one first opened the door, of stepping out onto a covered balcony. The glazed window faced west, so he could catch the sunsets. The sun was low now, the sky painted in purple and gold. At his home in the mountains, most of the windows faced east, affording him views of the sunrise. Something in him needed both the greeting and the goodbye of the sun. He'd always been drawn to sunlight, maybe because fire was his element to call, to control.

He checked his internal time: four minutes until sundown. Without checking the sunrise tables every day, he knew exactly when the sun would slide behind the mountains. He didn't own an alarm clock. He didn't need one. He was so acutely attuned to the sun's position that he had only to check within himself to know the time. As for waking at a particular time, he was one of those people who could tell himself to wake at a certain time, and he did. That talent had nothing to do with being Raintree, so he didn't have to hide it; a lot of perfectly ordinary people had the same ability.

He had other talents and abilities, however, that did require careful shielding. The long days of summer instilled in him an almost sexual high, when he could feel contained power buzzing just beneath his skin. He had to be doubly careful not to cause candles to leap into flame just by his presence, or to start wildfires with a glance in the dry-as-tinder brush. He loved Reno; he didn't want to burn it down. He just felt so damn *alive* with all the sunshine pouring down that he wanted to let the energy pour through him instead of holding it inside.

This must be how his brother Gideon felt while pulling lightning, all that hot power searing through his muscles, his veins. They had this in common, the connection with raw power. All the members of the farflung Raintree clan had some power, some heightened ability, but only members of the royal family could channel and control the earth's natural energies.

Dante wasn't just of the royal family, he was the Dranir, the leader of the entire clan. "Dranir" was synonymous with king, but the position he held wasn't ceremonial, it was one of sheer power. He was the oldest son of the previous Dranir, but he would have been passed over for the position if he hadn't also inherited the power to hold it.

Behind him came Al's distinctive knock on the door. The outer office was empty, Dante's secretary having gone home hours before. "Come in," he called, not turning from his view of the sunset.

The door opened, and Al said, "Mr. Raintree, this is Lorna Clay."

Dante turned and looked at the woman, all his senses on alert. The first thing he noticed was the vibrant color of her hair, a rich, dark red that encompassed a multitude of shades from copper to burgundy. The warm amber light danced along the iridescent strands, and he felt a hard tug of sheer lust in his gut. Looking at her hair was almost like looking at fire, and he had the same reaction.

The second thing he noticed was that she was spitting mad.

EVERLASTING LOVE™

Every great love has a story to tell™

If you're a romantic at heart, you'll definitely want to read this new series.

Available April 24

The Marriage Bed by Judith Arnold

An emotional story about a couple's love that
is put to the test when the shocking truth of
a long-buried secret comes to the surface.

&

Family Stories by Tessa McDermid

A couple's epic love story is pieced together
by their granddaughter in time for their
seventy-fifth anniversary.

And look for

The Scrapbook by Lynnette Kent

&

When Love Is True by Joan Kilby

from Harlequin® Everlasting Love™ this June.

Pick up a book today!

REQUEST YOUR FREE BOOKS!

2 FREE NOVELS PLUS 2 FREE GIFTS!

HARLEQUIN®

Blaze®

Red-hot reads!

YES! Please send me 2 FREE Harlequin® Blaze® novels and my 2 FREE gifts. After receiving them, if I don't wish to receive any more books, I can return the shipping statement marked "cancel." If I don't cancel, I will receive 6 brand-new novels every month and be billed just $3.99 per book in the U.S., or $4.47 per book in Canada, plus 25¢ shipping and handling per book and applicable taxes, if any*. That's a savings of at least 15% off the cover price! I understand that accepting the 2 free books and gifts places me under no obligation to buy anything. I can always return a shipment and cancel at any time. Even if I never buy another book from Harlequin, the two free books and gifts are mine to keep forever.

151 HDN EF3W   351 HDN EF3X

Name _____ (PLEASE PRINT)

Address _____ Apt. _____

City _____ State/Prov. _____ Zip/Postal Code _____

Signature (if under 18, a parent or guardian must sign)

Mail to the Harlequin Reader Service®:
IN U.S.A.: P.O. Box 1867, Buffalo, NY 14240-1867
IN CANADA: P.O. Box 609, Fort Erie, Ontario L2A 5X3

Not valid to current Harlequin Blaze subscribers.

Want to try two free books from another line?
Call 1-800-873-8635 or visit www.morefreebooks.com.

* Terms and prices subject to change without notice. NY residents add applicable sales tax. Canadian residents will be charged applicable provincial taxes and GST. This offer is limited to one order per household. All orders subject to approval. Credit or debit balances in a customer's account(s) may be offset by any other outstanding balance owed by or to the customer. Please allow 4 to 6 weeks for delivery.

Your Privacy: Harlequin is committed to protecting your privacy. Our Privacy Policy is available online at www.eHarlequin.com or upon request from the Reader Service. From time to time we make our lists of customers available to reputable firms who may have a product or service of interest to you. If you would prefer we not share your name and address, please check here. ☐

HB07

Romantic SUSPENSE

**Sparked by Danger,
Fueled by Passion.**

*This month and every month look for
four new heart-racing romances
set against a backdrop of suspense!*

Available in May 2007

Safety in Numbers
(*Wild West Bodyguards miniseries*)
by **Carla Cassidy**

Jackson's Woman
by **Maggie Price**

Shadow Warrior
(*Night Guardians miniseries*)
by **Linda Conrad**

One Cool Lawman
by **Diane Pershing**

Available wherever you buy books!

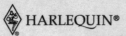

COMING NEXT MONTH

#321 BEYOND SEDUCTION Kathleen O'Reilly
The Red Choo Diaries, Bk. 3
The last thing respected talk-show host Sam Porter wants is to be the subject of a sex blog—but that's exactly what happens when up-and-coming writer Mercedes Brooks gets hold of him...and never wants to let him go!

#322 THE EX-GIRLFRIENDS' CLUB Rhonda Nelson
Ben Wilder is stunned when he discovers a Web site dedicated to bashing him. Sure, he's a little wild. So what? Then he learns Eden Rutherford, his first love, is behind the site, and decides some payback is in order. And he's going to start by showing Eden *exactly* what she's been missing....

#323 THE MAN TAMER Cindi Myers
It's All About Attitude...
Can't get your man to behave? Columnist Rachel Westover has the answer: man taming, aka behavior modification. Too bad she can't get Garret Kelly to obey. Sure, he's hers to command between the sheets, but outside...well, there might be something to be said for going wild!

#324 DOUBLE DARE Tawny Weber
Audra Walker is the ultimate bad girl. And to prove it, she takes a friend's dare—to hit on the next guy who comes through the door of the bar. Lucky for her, the guy's a definite hottie. Too bad he's also a cop....

#325 KISS AND DWELL Kelley St. John
The Sexth Sense, Bk. 1
Monique Vicknair has a secret—she and her family are mediums, charged with the job of helping lost souls cross over. But when Monique discovers her next assignment is sexy Ryan Chappelle, the last thing she wants to do is send him away. Because Ryan is way too much man to be a ghost....

#326 HOT FOR HIM Sarah Mayberry
Secret Lives of Daytime Divas, Bk. 3
Beating her rival for a coveted award has put Claudia Dostis on top. But when Leandro Mandalor challenges her to address the sizzle between them, her pride won't let her back down. In this battle for supremacy the gloves—and a lot of other clothes—are coming off!

www.eHarlequin.com

HBCNM0407